BEYOND

THE BOSS

THE ADVENTURES OF HORC:

BOOK 3

BY DREW SEREN

See what Drew Seren is up to.
Visit his website www.drewseren.com
And sign up for his newsletter

Copyright 2018 © MysticHawker Press
http://www.mystichawker.com/

ISBN: 978-1-945632-40-2

Edited by Robert Brownson
Cover design by Anadia-chan
www.anadia-chan.com

1

IGNORING THE leaden feeling of his arms, Alan Gosling shoved against the strangely heavy lid of his gaming pod, trying to move it out of the way. No one had responded to his initial tapping. He knew his pod had been moved from where it his house had fallen in on it after the tornado destroyed his neighborhood. There should be someone around. Techs, staff, someone. A hiss sounded and the lid of the pod finally opened; and the unresponsive game menu above him went dark. Fresh air flooded in on him, making him shiver from the cold in the strange room.

"What's going on?" His voice was hoarse as it rattled out of his dry throat. He'd never had a dry throat when coming out of his pod before. He normally emerged refreshed after a few hours of gaming.

A woman put a hand on his shoulder and tried to push him back into the pod. "Mr. Gosling, you need to take it slow. You've been physically inactive for a while now."

"No." Alan shook his head and tried to sit up. The bright room swam in his vision and, as much as he didn't want to, Alan sank back into the pod and let the ergonomic pillow embrace him. He hoped his head would clear soon. He wasn't supposed to be there.

"Here." The woman slowly came into focus. Between her voice and her brown hair cut into a bob cut, she could only be Miranda, Horc's sometimes guide, and more often irritating link to the real world and updater.

"You need a bit of sugar and caffeine to help you focus." She pushed a cold plastic cup into his hand.

"I don't need something to drink. I need to get back in there." His throat was almost too dry to force out the words. He'd never been in a pod for days on end, and his body wasn't happy about it. Sitting back up slowly, as to not make the room spin again, he brought the cup to his lips. The bubbly liquid tasted more like a thick syrup than soda, but it did help the dryness he was suffering.

"I'm sorry you can't go back in. We're locking down the servers to keep players out. The AI is just too dangerous at the moment." Miranda walked away from the pod and glanced at a monitor on a table a few feet away. "There are still way too many players in there."

"That's why I have to go back in," Alan objected. "I have to help them get out." He had friends in there and he didn't, couldn't abandon them.

Miranda shook her head again, her short hair dancing around her neck as she turned and walked back to the pod. "Nobody's ever spent as much time in game as you just did. We need to run some tests to make sure there aren't any lasting effects."

Alan finished off his drink and set the plastic cup on the side of his pod. "I don't have time for tests… my friends don't have time for me to undergo testing." He thought about the people still trapped in the game. Sure, Greensleeves, who had become Bigdaddybear, Baladara, Tufkakes, and a few others could still log out, but Slasher and more were locked by the AI. They had no idea if the AI had figured out the loophole they had exploited to get captives free. If it had, they were going to have to work out something. But that was for the designers like Miranda and Rick to work out from the outside. He needed to be in the game helping people stay alive until they could log out. It was true that he'd been stuck in there for almost a week after the tornado destroyed his house and made his pod malfunction, but he wasn't about to sit around waiting for something to happen when he could be in there helping his friends and co-workers.

A phone rang nearby. Miranda reached into the pocket of her white lab coat and pulled out a smartphone. She tapped it and held it up to her ear. A frown crossed her face. "Yes, we got him… He seems fine, but we won't know until we run tests… He's wanting to go back in to help people get out… I have to object…" she turned away from Alan and took a few steps away from his pod.

Alan strained to hear her side of the conversation.

Miranda tensed and clenched her hand that wasn't holding the phone. She paced farther away, although her voice rose and Alan caught words like "No… Can't… die… my… responsibility…" She all but shouted the word "Fine" then she yanked the phone away from her face and acted like she was about to throw it before jamming it back into her pocket.

She sighed heavily, then turned back to Alan. "I would like to do a basic physical on you quickly before we return you to the game."

Alan grinned. "Thank you." He swung his legs over the side of the pod, then realized he was naked. He always striped down to go into his pod, but so much had happened, his state of undress had slipped his mind.

As if anticipating his needs, Miranda picked up a pair of scrub pants from a table next to the pod and handed them to him. "I'll try to make this as fast as possible."

"I appreciate this." Alan pulled the pants up. They were a little tighter than he liked, but weren't so snug as to cut off his circulation.

Miranda walked over to the terminal on the desk and hit a couple of keys on the keyboard.

When Alan put his feet on the cold tile floor and started to stand, his legs went weak and he grabbed hold of the side of the pod to keep from falling.

"I was expecting some muscle weakness," Miranda said, grabbing a rolling chair and swinging it close to him. "Take a seat while I wait for my assistants to get in here."

Alan grabbed the arms of the chair and hoped it didn't roll as he eased himself into it. His arms felt like they were going to give out too, but they weren't as weak as his legs. He managed to get into the padded seat. Although it wasn't overly graceful, his plop would've been a complete sprawl if the chair had moved when he'd been trying to land.

Seconds after he straightened in the chair, a door opened, and two more people in white lab coats hurried in.

"Sorry, Miranda, we didn't get the notification he was out," the man said with a thick Texas accent. Hearing it reinforced to Alan that he was near the office, and not whisked off to some other state.

"We were getting lunch," the woman added. Her light brown skin tones marked her as of Hispanic descent, although her accent was pure Middle American. "I thought we had time for a bite before he woke up."

"So did I," Miranda replied as she turned from the cabinet she'd walked over to. She dropped a couple of things on a rolling metal tray like Alan had seen at the dentist's office during his recent cleaning several months earlier. "He's recovered quickly and will be going back in."

The man stopped and stared from Alan to Miranda. "Going back in? That isn't safe. We don't know what a week in the pod has done to him."

Miranda sighed. "Not my call. He wants to go help save his friends."

After running a long-fingered hand through his short red hair, the man shook his head. "Dude, you're a sucker for punishment, aren't you?"

Alan flashed him a smile and shrugged. "My mom told me that for years as I was growing up."

"We're going to get some vitals and blood work," Miranda said, without looking in Alan's direction. "Do what we can to keep him alive, and that's all we can do."

Alan was torn. He hated being pushy enough to upset someone, but they all needed to understand that he had friends still stuck in Halfworld and he wasn't about to give up on them when they needed him.

"Look, there's a couple of things we need in there, beyond just getting me back to the party." Alan held out his arm as Miranda approached with a blood pressure cuff.

"Like what?" Miranda wrapped the cuff around his upper arm. "Hold still."

"Right before I got yanked, we realized we'd stopped getting XP. We need to be higher levels to take on the AI, particularly in its dragon form."

Miranda pursed her lips as the cuff reached its tightest point then slowly began to release. She didn't say anything until it was over. "Not really my area of expertise. I'm a pod technician. I make sure things don't malfunction to the point of killing people, and you came very close to dying, Mr. Gosling."

"You need to talk to the game designers about that," the man said. "We can get them on a conference call with you so they can see what they can work out."

"But we have to make sure you're fit first," Miranda snapped.

"We need blood." The woman stepped close with a syringe.

Giving blood was something Alan hated, but he held as still as possible while turning his head so he didn't have to watch thhe needle enter his skin.

ALAN RUBBED his arm, careful not to dislodge the Band-Aid covering the hole in the crook of his elbow. He'd stayed still and quiet as they poked, prodded, measured, and weighed him. Miranda might've been referring to it as a cursory exam, but it was the most thorough physical Alan could remember having in his life.

"Okay, you can talk to the developers while I get the tests results," Miranda said.

"I've got the conference call set up for you," the male assistant said from the desk.

"Thanks." Alan still didn't know the names of either of the two who'd come in from lunch to help Miranda, it made them almost like NPCs.

He managed to walk over to the terminal and settle into the chair. His legs were feeling stronger the longer he was out of the pod. Miranda seemed pleased by that, but there wasn't much else she was pleased about from what Alan could tell.

There were four windows up on the monitor. Three of them had people facing the cameras, while the other showed an empty chair.

"We're waiting for Rick to get back," the large pale man with gray hair said from the upper left box. "Since you've already met him, why don't we do introductions while we wait? I'm Paul Rivers from the LA office, head of AI development."

"I'm Lilly Goldstein," the blonde woman in the lower right box said. "I'm also out of the LA office, chief NPC programmer."

"And I'm Neal Punjabi," the dark-haired, dark-eyed man in the upper-right window said in a thick Hindi accent. "Project coordinator. I must tell you, Mr. Gosling, we are so very sorry for the malfunction of your pod, and your ordeal in the game."

Alan shook his head. "The pod saved my life. From what I've heard, if I hadn't been in it, the house would've collapsed on top of me, so I'm not mad about that. What I am worried about is the AI malfunctioning."

"Actually, it's not exactly malfunctioning," Rivers said. "It's one of the most advanced AIs ever programmed. It's supposed to learn. We just didn't anticipate it learning negative things."

Alan chocked back a laugh. "Negative things is one way to put what it's learning. You do realize that it's locked our party for XP. It's kidnapping players and forcing them to fight in an arena, and now has taken some of those kidnapped players hostage so you won't be able to shut down the game. I think that all qualifies as negative things."

Rivers frowned. "There's more to it than that."

"Wait a minute," Goldstein interrupted him. "What do you mean it's put in a level cap for your party? That shouldn't be possible. Things dealing with players accounts are controlled through a system the AI doesn't have access to."

"Players accounts shouldn't be blocked from logging out either." Alan felt a minor headache coming on. Although he wasn't used to dealing with programmers, he was more accustomed to dealing with corporate people who had little or no idea what was going on in their departments. If these were the heads of departments, they might not have a clear clue as to what the AI's capabilities really were. People like Rick were the ones he really needed to be talking to.

"We think it learned that from your experience," Punjabi said. "We're still trying to figure out what exactly happened in your pod to block you from logging out, but it's entirely possible that while we were trying to figure out how to access your pod and override that function of it that the AI followed our tracks."

"And then applied our findings to other players' accounts." A large well-tanned man appeared in the empty window. He looked enough like the avatar for Rick that had driven Horc and the party from Tragiczan to the coast that Alan was sure it was Rick. "Hi, Alan, sorry I was late. I was texting with David. The party is on their way back to the mainland while we're trying to track the AI's dragon avatar."

"Did you let him know I'd be back with them shortly?" Alan wanted to wrap up the conference call so he could log back in and lend a hand.

"You'll be the last person we allow to log in," Rick said grimly. "I'm trying to work out a way for an admin override on your level. If you can wait on that, I think I can give you a bit of an edge."

Alan hated the idea of delaying his return to Halfworld, but if a short delay would give him an edge, he'd be willing to do it.

"He could use a little real-world rest," Miranda said from behind him. "His tests are showing signs of stress, which is to be expected. But he's in surprisingly good shape otherwise. The pods are working the way they're supposed to, supporting the body even when the stay is unexpectedly extended."

Turning slightly, so he could glare at her, Alan added, "And he's sitting right here, you don't have to talk about me in third person."

Miranda shrugged.

"Remington, what has your team been able to determine as far as the AI's location in the game?" Rivers asked.

Rick glanced at something just on the other side of the camera. "As far as we can tell, it's actually still on the move, heading into higher level zones. These are places where lower level characters won't be able to survive simple encounters, let alone something like the AI itself."

"So that's why we need the level boost, or something to give us at least a chance of surviving." Alan tried to think of what he would do to give characters a chance of defeating a massively powerful monster. "Better equipment would be nice, but we have to be careful with that one. In the arena there was some kind of magic there that blocked all the magic bonuses our weapons had. We were able to use potions and such, just not the magical adds on our gear."

A line of perplexion appeared on Punjabi's forehead. "Why would it think to negate a magical weapon? We didn't design it to think that way."

"But we did," Rick countered. "We used every fantasy book, movie, music, or game created in the past hundred years, and then some, for its programming. We didn't worry about some of the more morality-based works, because it's a game. Why would we need to worry about morality in a game?"

Alan closed his eyes and sighed. "I thought most AIs were built… ah, programed with a sense of morality. This thing is interacting with real people. You're telling me that none of the NPCs in the game understand the basic things like not cheating players, or having consistent prices for goods, or even being honest, as long as that's who they're supposed to be?"

"No, you don't understand how this whole thing works," Goldstein objected, combing her fingers through her hair, then picking up a pencil from her desk and chewing on it. "The NPCs were programmed separately from the AI. They were integrated with it. They shouldn't be able to deviate from their base programing. Sure, they can differ their responses and actions depending on how the players interact with them. If they couldn't, the game wouldn't be that much more advanced than games from fifty years ago."

Her response explained why Horc had been able to convince Caleb Sureshot to let him keep Wolf, when all the companions caught during the quests were supposed to vanish and be returned to where they'd come from. Sureshot and the other NPCs were adaptable to a point.

"But the AI has shown an ability to conscript NPCs to do his bidding," Rick said. "Otherwise the Pirates in Tragiczan wouldn't have been kidnapping people and taking them to the arena." He paused and rubbed his chin. "And it deliberately led Horc there with quests. This isn't good. It's already manipulating the NPCs and we didn't even realize it."

Goldstein chewed on her pencil. "But that shouldn't be possible. If the AI was trying to manipulate the NPCs, they'd be acting up, be jerky and such. So far there've been no reports of that. Not to mention that it doesn't understand programming, unless someone fed it coding books."

Punjabi and Rivers both shook their heads.

"Why would any of the AI programing team feed the AI coding books?" Punjabi asked first. "It would serve no purpose and simply take up memory that could be allotted to something more practical."

Alan raised a hand. "Guys, this is all really interesting, but it's not solving the problem at hand. Your AI is out of control and it could potentially kill someone. We need to get all the people it has hostage out of the game. Then the rest of the free players can log out so you can bring that game down. How are we going to accomplish this?"

His words seemed to hit a nerve and for almost a minute, none of them said a word.

Rick spoke first. "I agree with Alan…Mr. Gosling. We need to get folks out, then we can spend time going over the AI's code with a fine-tooth comb."

Punjabi frowned and then turned as if talking to someone just off the camera. "Right. I'm going to get my team working on finding a way to override the AI without bringing down the game. If we can do that, we can get everyone out safely, then bring the system down."

"Okay." Rick nodded sagely. "While you do that, I'm going to get my team working to find ways to get the members of Horc's party strong enough to storm the dragon's lair. Maybe if you can't bypass the AI, we can defeat it. If it's been programmed with lots of fantasy knowledge and has taken a dragon as its avatar, then if we defeat it, maybe we can win."

"I'll help you with that," Goldstein said. "Maybe some of what we've programmed the NPCs with can be useful in this."

"Any help you can give will be greatly appreciated." Rick made a note on a pad next to his keyboard.

"Good." Rivers tapped on a pad on his desk. "Sounds like we've got a plan. Everyone check in with me as we make progress. Remington, since you're in contact with your husband in the game, you can be our go-between for Mr. Gosling's party."

"I can do that," Rick agreed.

"Good. You and Bordeaux get Gosling back in the game as quickly as possible, but as strong as possible." Rivers looked toward Alan's window. "Remington, see if you can boost the rest of Gosling's party too. Let's get this thing shut down. Also, Gosling, make sure your party understands that none of this gets out to the public. News of a rogue game AI could shut us down faster than a politician can lie."

Alan wondered how dedicated his friends were to Total Immersion Systems. If any of them weren't willing to toe the corporate line, there wasn't much he could do about that. He just nodded to Rivers, not wanting to rock the boat. He was going to be able to get back in the game, and that was all that mattered at that point.

2

ALAN STRETCHED and yawned. The pillow didn't feel right. Then as consciousness hit him full force, he remembered he wasn't in his bed, but a bed in the pod lab. He jerked up and looked around. No one was in the room. There weren't any windows, clocks or monitors, so he had no idea how long he'd been asleep. He'd only lain down because Rick had asked for a little time to get things set up before he went back into the game.

All he had on were the scrubs Miranda had given him. It hit him that with his house destroyed, he didn't have any clothes of his own. The borrowed pants were the closest thing he had to anything in life, other than his pod. He wondered if there were other things that survived in the rubble of his home. Once he had everyone out of the game, he was going to need to take time and see what he could find. After that, he was going to have to file a report with his insurance company and wait for them to get back to him.

With a sigh, he put his head in his hands. There was so much he needed to do, but it could all wait until he made sure everyone was safely out of the game. Sure, there were other people who might be able to do the job, but he had a connection with Slasher in the game. IRL he was just another corporate bigwig at Total Immersion Systems whom Alan had never met, but that didn't matter.

"Hey, the monitor said you were awake." The man who assisted Miranda walked in with a tray that had a couple of brightly colored bottles on it. "Miranda said your electrolytes were a bit low according to your blood work, so she wants you to have a couple of sports drinks before you go back in."

Alan frowned. He wasn't a big enough gamer or jock to enjoy energy drinks, but he figured they couldn't hurt if his body was short of important nutrients. "Any word from Rick?"

The man looked confused for a moment. "Rick? Oh, you mean Mr. Remington. I'm Fred by the way. Yeah, he called a few minutes ago and said he had things set up when you were ready to go back in."

"And you guys didn't wake me?" Alan tried not to glare, it was probably not Fred's fault he hadn't been woken. The energy drink didn't taste as syrupy as the drink the previous night had.

"Was working on that. I had the drinks out of the fridge when Miranda told me your monitor showed you awake." Fred set the tray down on the bedside table. "Honestly, I can't believe you're going back in. They're saying they've got most of the players out at this point, only a couple of dozen or so left in, and over half of those can't log out."

Alan finished of the first drink and reached for the second one. He really hoped Miranda wasn't going to make him eat something before he went back in the pod. The pods were designed to keep the players alive with a nutrient feed if they were in there too long. He was probably just thirsty because his pod had been running low on supplies or something like that.

"I know some of those who can't log out. That's all the reason I need for going back in. If I can rescue them, we'll all get out and the AI can be shut down and reprogramed." The second drink was almost refreshing. Alan wished Fred had brought another in.

"Sounds fair."

Before Fred could say more, the door opened again, and Miranda walked in. She wasn't moving as angrily as she had the previous night, but there was still a heaviness in her footfalls that was more than a woman her size should have.

"I'm still against this, but Remington assures me he's going to equip you the best he can. We've also made some modifications to one of our newer model pods that should at least protect you from having the AI attack the pod controls." She stopped a few feet away from Alan and put her hands behind her back. The move looked more like she was trying to do something with them to hide her anger.

"So I won't be using my pod?" Alan finished off the second bottle and handed it to Fred.

Miranda shook her head. "We're still analyzing your pod, trying to figure out what went wrong. It's not safe at this point."

"But I *will* get it back?" If he lost his pod too, everything really would be gone.

"The company may issue you an upgraded model as a replacement." She sighed. "The final decision hasn't been made on that."

"Okay, so when can I go back in?" Alan stood, feeling stronger than before he had gone to sleep.

Miranda looked like she really wanted to argue with him. "Remington wants to talk to you first. You can vidcall him from my monitor in the other room."

Alan walked to the door, trying to remember the way to Miranda's lab. "Thanks." The tile floor was so cold that he was a little surprised they hadn't provided him with some socks, or paper booties, or something. The AC was more than a little brisk as he walked down the hall toward the lab. The lack of other people in the area made him wonder if it was night, or with the threats about going to the media, if that area of the building had been cut off to everyone but Miranda and her team.

"Mr. Gosling, if you would slow down, I can open the doors for you." Miranda hustled to keep up with Alan's longer legs.

"Thank you, Miranda." Alan slowed down just a little. He didn't want to show too much compliance to her.

"I know we can't totally stop you… okay, we could, but corporate management wants you to try to get folks out. It'll look a lot better for them if we've just had a few people lost in a game for a couple of days, rather than people dying in the game."

Alan nodded as they approached the door to Miranda's lab. "Having people die would be a major nightmare for the marketing folks. It might also cause the stocks to crash and the company to go under. I like my job enough that I don't want to be finding another one."

Miranda held her ID badge to the reader on the side of the door. There was a soft click, and the door opened. "That's probably the reason they're sending you back in."

"Right." Alan walked over to the desk where the monitor was up and a com window was open, Rick sat in view of the camera on the other end.

"Ah, Alan." Rick flashed a warm welcoming smile. "I heard you'd woken up. Good timing, I had just finished the adjustments to the player interface to be able to give you a bumped up character and send you in with the weapons and armor to help the rest of the party."

Alan frowned as the words sank in. "Bumped up character? Won't we be able to just increase Horc to the point we need him to be?" Although Alan had started his toon using completely random character generation, he was comfortable with what Horc could do. There wasn't anything he really wanted to change in the character other than making him strong enough to stand up to the dragon.

Rick shook his head. "It's like the folks who were able to get out of the arena by dying and logging out in those couple of seconds before the AI could take control of them again. The AI knows Horc. If you go back in, it will instantly recognize you. We need to make some changes."

Alan leaned back in the chair. He really didn't want to make changes. "What are you thinking?"

"There's a couple of possibilities…a Half Troll, for example. Still powerful, still dangerous, if you go with any kind of caster."

Alan shook his head. "I'd rather not go in with a caster. From what Mike and David have said, casters can be fairly complex. I need the character to be fairly simple and direct. That's why I like the Ranger. Not big on tanking characters either."

Rick let out a long breath. "Ranger limits us a bit. How do you feel about a Half Elf?"

"Helf the Ranger? Sounds odd. Horc is a better name."

"You wouldn't have to name it Helf, you could go with just about anything at this point on this server."

"What if we just changed the name and the level, would that confuse the AI enough?" Alan had an idea come to him.

"Horc2.0…" Rick rubbed the bridge of his nose, then shrugged. "Maybe. So far we don't have any characters with numbers in their names; that will come as the server gets more crowded."

Horc2.0 sounded a little silly, and clinical to Alan. He was going in as a corporate lackey, a spy of sorts, but it was a rescue mission. "Horc007, it's more digits in the name and a dot in a name might give it away as something special, so I'd rather not use one."

Rick thought about it for a moment, then nodded. "It might work. But you're going to stick with your race and class?"

"You're changing my level, so let's hope two changes will be sufficient to confuse it." Alan wasn't familiar enough with AIs to know what it was going to take to make it hard for the thing to not spot him when he re-entered the game.

"Depends on how much it's learned over the past ten days."

"Wait…what? It's been ten days?" Alan asked. Miranda had been fairly pushy about not telling him how long he'd been in the pod, and he wasn't about to admit to her that he'd lost track of time in the game. He glanced to the side where Miranda had pulled up a chair next to him.

She glared at the monitor. "Remington, you weren't supposed to tell him that."

Rick shrugged. "Someone needed to. But at this point, that's neither here nor there. Okay, we're also going to change up some of your specializations. You've been using sword or axe, you're now going to use pole arms."

"Okay." Alan wasn't sure what that would do. "But I still get my bow?"

"Yeah. We've had problems with crossbows and guns as far as programming go. The guns are as apt to blow up as shoot and crossbows tend to be difficult to master, so we're keeping you with a bow. I'm thinking we can get you a tiger, or lion for a companion."

Alan shook his head. He still couldn't explain it, but he'd bonded to Wolf. He didn't want a different companion. "No. I'm keeping my wolf."

"I was afraid you'd say that, and David said you wouldn't agree to that, so I have an idea on how to upgrade Wolf and keep him a wolf." Rick pursed his lips.

"It'll take me a couple of hours after you log back in to get him to you, but I'll make it happen."

That made Alan feel a little better. "Thanks."

"Okay, now your armor is going to upgrade to chainmail with a resistance to dragon fire."

"Wait… the AI has figured out how to breathe fire?" A fire-breathing AI dragon sounded really scary, but with what Alan had found out about the programming of the AI, it made sense that the thing would have some kind of breath weapon.

"We don't know that for sure," Rick replied. "It might spit acid or use noxious clouds. Hard to say what it's doing. We're only able to track the thing through the players it's grabbed, and then only on a limited basis. We can't tell if they're in a cave, a dungeon, a citadel, or what; we just know where they are on the map."

Alan shrugged. "Sort of like when we tracked them to the arena."

"A little worse." Rick picked up a stylus and tapped it on the table. "It looks like the AI's separating the people. They are scattered over the northern half of the continent."

A sinking feeling hit Alan. "That's going to make it really hard to break in and rescue everyone at one time."

"We know. I think a concentrated attack on the AI might be the answer. I'm working with Rivers, Punjabi, and Goldstein on coming up with a real plan for the assault. By the time you get there, things should be sorted out."

A soft, sarcastic smile crept across Alan's face. "And most plans fall apart as soon as the enemy's engaged. When I get back with the others, we'll work on something too. David can keep you informed on what we come up with."

"That's a good plan." Rick gave him a huge grin. "Okay. One other thing we're recommending you do as a group; go beyond being a party and form a guild. You'll have to go to one of the starting zone cities for that, the party's nearly back to Tragiczan, so Red Wind Terrace isn't far away. You and the other Orc Neutrals go in, set it up and when you get back to the rest of the party get them to join."

After what had happened the last time they split the party, Alan didn't like that idea. "If you're going to be giving everyone level boost to help bypass the AI, can you also go in and make everyone neutral? It would make things easier to stay together."

Rick's stylus tapping increased, then he nodded. "That makes sense. We'll add that to the upgrade package we force down on everyone. To be honest, we're not sure how the upgrade is going to impact the people in-game."

"Impact? In what way?" Alan knew from personal experience how some of the toying with things while players were running their toons could hurt.

"Pain, short periods of disorientation, black outs." Rick counted things off on his fingers.

"If they're somewhere safe when it happens, it shouldn't be a problem." Alan sighed. "But if they happen to be in combat at the time, it could be disastrous."

Rick nodded. "Since we've been pulling players from the game, we haven't had anyone die in combat after the arena, but there's a chance it might give the AI more prisoners."

The door to the lab burst open, and Fred rushed in with the woman who'd been with him earlier trailing him.

"Miranda, we've got a problem." He thrust a pad at her. "We just got notification of someone dying in one of the pods."

Miranda yanked the pad out of his hands and as she scanned the screen, the color faded from her face.

For several seconds no one said a word. Miranda closed her eyes and took a heavy breath.

She opened her eyes. "It was one of the people whose player profile was locked by the AI. Accounts are it was a heart attack. Odds are the AI did something. We're out of time."

"I'll let the others know." Rick started to turn away, then looked back at the camera. "Alan, you don't have to do this. It's too risky."

Alan shook his head. "Riiiight. So from here on out, nobody dies." Knowing that all of his party had died at least once, and he'd come really close several times, that sounded like the game was going to be a lot harder than it had been. Alan realized the stakes were higher than ever. When he got back in the game, not only was he going to need to rescue people, he was going to have to make sure his party stayed alive through the whole thing, or they were going to need to be rescued too before they died in their pods at the hands of the rogue AI. Yeah, the shit just got real.

3

THE SLIGHT bit of disorientation Alan felt as he re-entered Halfworld vanished as Horc looked around. The familiar tents of Tragiczan filled his view. The vendors were there, but things were a lot quieter than they had been previously. There weren't any calls to sell wares. For the most part the NPCs were standing around as if they were waiting for instructions.

"Kinda creepy, isn't it?" Baladara walked up to Horc and grinned. "Although we can still interact with the NPCs, buy things, sell things, get rooms, that sort of things, they've stopped soliciting interactions."

The text over Baladara's head read **Baladara, Human, Mage, Level 48**. It brought a little smile to Horc. Rick had been able to give everyone a boost.

Bigdaddybear, Tufkakes, Stanoran, and Theodore were all there, also raised to level forty eight. The weapons and armor everyone had looked shiny and new. There were several other people standing around whom Horc didn't recognize.

"I wonder what the AI's done to them to cause this." Horc walked up to a fruit vendor who was staring straight ahead with a vacant look. "Hello."

She blinked. "Hi, what kind of fruit would you like today?"

Horc shook his head. "Nothing for me, thanks."

"Yeah, and then we get responses like that," Tufkakes said as the fruit vendor again fell silent and stared into the distance.

"It started about halfway across the ocean," Bigdaddybear said. "Captain Calamity stopped talking our ears off, just grabbed hold of his steering wheel and didn't say anything until we reached the pier at Dustbinnia, then it was just shouting to get off his boat."

"I wonder if that would coincide with when the AI dragon reached its lair," Horc stepped away from the fruit vendor and scanned the rest of the small encampment. "I don't know if this is going to make things easier or harder."

"Depends on what we need," Baladara said with a shrug. "If we just need basic supplies, it'll make things a little easier, not so much back and forth, but if we don't know exactly what we're going to need, then we won't be getting suggestions and such. It's suddenly reminding me of some old MMOs I used to play as a kid. Those were the good old days, but compared to today's games, rather boring."

"Right." Horc hoped up on an empty vendor cart. The big Orc standing next to it didn't say a word. It wasn't right. Before the AI started acting up, the thing would've, at the very least, been shouting at him and hitting him, at worst would've pulled the big nasty-looking sword out of his belt and attacked Horc with it. "Okay everyone, I've got some announcements."

The party, and the people Horc didn't know stared at him. There were probably a dozen new people, all total, with a good variety of races and classes.

"First, unless you didn't realize it, the game has turned deadly. Right before I logged back in, the folks in the pod lab got notification that someone had died of a heart attack while in their pod." He paused as a couple of people gasped. "Not surprisingly, they are one of the people currently being held by the AI in its dragon form. With that said, we're all in danger here. If that one death was just the AI testing its power, we're pretty sure it was a successful test."

A man in the back of the group, Rambull, a huge Minotorian Shaman, raised his hoof-like hand. "Do we know why the AI has turned against us? Shouldn't it be programed not to do this?"

"From what the developers told me before they let me back in, they don't know, that's why they have to bring the game down so they can analyze the AI and figure out what's wrong before the game goes live. Yes, it should be programed to not act the way it is." Horc didn't bother elaborating about the potentially faulty programming. "I came back to do what I can to get the players the AI has taken hostage free, so they can log out and escape the game. Once everyone is free, then we all log out and the game comes down."

Another hand went up, a female Troll, Jamica, a Rogue. "It got my entire party when they died in the arena, what's to keep it from just killing us and taking us over?"

"Bigdaddybear is going to send a list of our player names to his husband, who's one of the programmers. Rick's going to go in and put everyone on a watch list. If for any reason we die in game, his team is going to help pull us out. Also if you die, be ready to hit log out as soon as you start to rez. It's a very small window for them to help us get out in that situation."

Jamica nodded her green head, the vibrant verdant dreadlocks rocked back and forth. "And what about this upgrade your party got. Can the rest of us get it? If we're facing certain death, it would be nice to go out in style."

Horc glanced at Bigdaddybear. "Can you check on that? It would be good to have the strongest party possible." He returned his attention to the gathered players. "The thing is, none of you need to stay in the game at this point. Sure, we'll appreciate all the help we can get in this adventure, but it's risky. If you want to log out now, nobody's going to think ill of you. Most of you probably have people IRL who are counting on you to be there for them. Also anyone not in a pod, although you appear safe from the AI takeovers, if you log out at any point, you won't be able to log back in; well, as far as logging back in, that goes for pod folks too."

"Looks like Lisa and I are going to be tag teaming this one," Baladara said from a few feet away.

"We're here for you, like you've been there for us," Titanya said with a raised fist.

Among the people Horc didn't know, several of them muttered, "I'm out of here," or "No way," then disappeared from the crowd.

Horc stood there on the vendor cart for a minute, not saying anything as the others stared at him. Then he did a quick head count. Including his party, they had ten players. "Okay, one of the first things we need to do is go to Red Wind Terrace. If you're not at least Orc neutral, Rick will take care of that when he updates your toons. We have to go set up a guild. In a guild, if we're fighting together we're going to get buffs to attacks and damage taken will be less."

"What if we're already part of a guild?" Jamica asked.

"Are you?" Horc asked.

The Troll shook her head. "No, but someone might be."

Horc looked over the crowd and no one seemed to make any indication they were part of a guild. "Looks like we're lucking out on this one. We are going to have to come up with a guild name, however."

"TK and I will work on that," Baladara said. "We both love naming things. Better than Theodore does."

Theodore shrugged. "I can't help it that names are one of my weaknesses."

"Obviously." Tufkakes laughed. "An Ursan named Ted, then you come back as Theodore, that's almost as bad as Horc007 up there."

Horc shook his head. "Please just stick with Horc, it was either something like 007 or 2.0 and I was afraid the AI would catch on to the 2.0 too easily."

Bigdaddybear raised his huge hairy arm. "Okay. Rick said he'll get to work on upgrading folks if we can get a list of people, so let's get this started. I'll warn you, there's a bit of disorientation when you get upgraded, a little worse than when you log in to the game. Goggle and Glove folks shouldn't have a problem." He glanced at Baladara at his side. "At least our bitchy Elf here didn't."

"You don't know that," Baladara quipped. "Maybe I just managed to hide it better than you guys did. At least I didn't pass out over it."

The new folks walked over to Bigdaddybear and started giving him their information for their upgrade. Even with the folks who'd left, they still had a decent sized party with a good variety of classes. With any luck, they just might get everyone saved and out of the game.

Horc glanced down at his side where Wolf should be. He hoped Rick wouldn't take too long getting his companion upgraded. It felt strange not having Wolf there with him. He hopped off the cart and walked among the other toons. They were looking at him to lead them. That was strange. Even though he was used to being a floor lead at work, this was different. Somehow helping techs give customers the right answer just wasn't the same as ten people trusting him to get them and a group of hostages through a game and home safely. He was going to do his best to not fail any of them.

4

IT DIDN'T take too long for Rick to get all the new party members upgraded. It took longer for some of them to recover from the disorientation of the boost than it did for him to level them up.

Rambull sat on the ground for nearly ten minutes before Horc walked over to him. "Dude, are you okay?"

The big Minotauren shook his head, and Horc jumped back to avoid being impaled on his long ivory colored horns. "It almost feels like he ran us through everything we could experience to get to level forty eight." He closed his big brown eyes and looked like he was about to throw up. "So much to take in."

"What level were you before the upgrade?" Horc couldn't remember from his glance at the player's name earlier.

"Five." Rambull put his head in his hands. "I probably shouldn't have been on the arena, but I had friends in the party who watched out for me while we made it to the island, then made sure nobody killed me in the arena. I put on almost two levels on in combat in the arena."

Tufkakes squatted down in front of him. "That took some balls, Dude. Why didn't you just stick with the starting zones?"

"Some friends said the arenas were fun. I didn't have tons of time to spend in game, and I'm just doing this for fun and the bonus money." Rambull shrugged. "I figured have fun and not worry about other things."

Horc paced a couple of steps away from the Shaman. "Okay. Then why didn't you log out when you had the chance? I don't guarantee this is going to be tons of fun."

"One of my coworkers was taken. He doesn't have anyone else in the world. I think he'd appreciate it if I was there. We're friends outside of work too." Rambull let out a long breath, put his hands on his knees and forced himself to his hooves. "Okay. I think I can do this."

"Good." Horc turned and looked at the other gathered players who'd recovered from their upgrades. "Alright folks, let's head to Red Wind Terrace so we can form our guild and get some buffs. Hopefully by then, Rick or one of the other developers will have figured out exactly where we need to go so we don't just wander off to the north and get lost."

Tufkakes laughed. "Never forget, 'Not all who wander are lost.'"

Baladara chuckled. "What TK said."

Not sure how he felt about the new level of buddyship between the two who'd started off on rough standing, Horc grinned. "Alright then, let's head out."

Without anyone disagreeing with him, he walked to the head of the group. Bigdaddybear, Titanya, Baladara, and Tufkakes fanned out at his sides. It wasn't the same as having Wolf there, but they were on their way.

THE HALBERD was awkward as Horc swung it at the Scalteon Scorpion. A swarm of six of the heavily armored arachnids that were the size of Volkswagen Bugs had hit the party, appearing out of the white sand dune that was the same color as their shells. It had been fast and furious. Horc was too close to fire his bow, so he relied on his new weapon, basically a spear with an axe blade just below the spear head. It was top heavy and took a lot of strength to swing it effectively.

The scorpion slid under his swing, and the momentum of the weapon kept going in a wide arc.

Baladara dropped to the hard-packed sand of the road as she got off a Fireball that finished off their assailant. "Hey, watch it."

"Sorry," Horc muttered as he turned for the next target.

Rambull was trying to take on one of the scorpions by himself. The thing had him down on the ground, and the Shaman's health was dropping quickly.

Holding the halberd like a lance, Horc charged the scorpion. He managed to hit it behind the head and roll it off Rambull. The hit was a good hard hit and knocked a decent chunk of the thing's health bar down, but it wasn't a critical hit. In the arena, he'd gotten to the point where he was doing critical hits on a regular basis, but the short fight with the scorpions didn't have any.

Bigdaddybear's blast of brown Druid magic hit the scorpion, followed by Baladara's next Fireball. The thing shuddered and died as its health bar flashed red and vanished. Seconds later the thing pixelated into the sand.

Horc stared at where the arachnid had been and rubbed his face. It had been the hardest fight he'd had since before they reached the arena, but there was something missing.

"Damn it," Tufkakes voice broke the strange silence that had settled over them. "These are like the others we encountered. No loot. What's going on?"

Bigdaddybear shook his head. "Only thing Rick and I can figure out is the AI's making it harder on us. Like these scorpions. They're at our level and there's enough of them to give us fits. That's not how this section of road was before. Last time we traveled this way, the scorpions and sandworms weren't as aggressive and were lower level. Halfworld shouldn't have auto adjusting mobs that make fighting harder the higher level you are. At this point it's supposed to have set levels in the different zones."

"In other words, we're screwed." Jamica wiped her daggers off as she slipped them back into the bandolier across her chest.

"As long as the numbers stay close to our own, we should be okay," Bigdaddybear said. "One plus to all of us being at level forty eight is the mobs can't be much higher than we are."

"That's right, level cap for the game is fifty," Theodore added. He wiped a hand across his head and plopped down on the road. "But that doesn't help much when we're not getting critical hits for anything."

"Okay, so it's not just me," Horc said, sliding his halberd out behind him so he could clean the bug guts off the spearhead and axe blade.

Baladara pulled out a flask and took a long drink. "Nope. We noticed it on the way to Tragiczan. Everything's more aggressive, not dropping loot, and harder to kill. We're not sure if the harder to kill bit is us or them."

"Maybe a combo of both," Rambull said, taking a drink of his own. "I'm on the development team that worked on the combat algorithms. If I had to guess, the mobs being upgraded, the AI's done something to their armor making it harder to get crits on them, and at the same time, it's doing something to take the critical edge off player's attacks."

With the last bit of grime off his weapon, Horc pointed the blade up and leaned it against his shoulder. It made a much better walking staff than it did a battle implement, or at least he thought so. "This isn't a good thing. It's going to make our fights all the harder. We need easier, not harder." He didn't like his games too easy, but if things got too hard, he'd have trouble helping his people stay alive.

"You're right there," Baladara agreed. "Now we need to get the info on where we need to go and how we need to get there. The sooner we can get out of this mess of a game, the better I'm going to like it."

"I thought you were the one who liked fantasy games." Horc flashed her a grin.

"When they aren't actively trying to kill me." Baladara shook the sand out of her robes. "So let's keep on the road and get as far as we can as fast as we can."

Horc glanced around at the party members cleaning their weapons and eating and drinking. They hadn't lost anyone, but most were at least down a bit in either health or mana, which explained the eating and drinking. "Everyone good?" He shouted. He wasn't exactly sure how to be party leader but figured one of the things he should do was make sure everyone was fine before they moved on down the road toward Red Wind Terrace.

He got a round of "Yeah." And thumbs up. Nobody seemed majorly the worse for wear.

"Good, let's keep going." Using his halberd as a hiking stick, Horc struck off down the road, trying to keep his eyes peeled for more mobs that were the same color as the sand, hoping nothing got the jump on them as they hiked along the desert road.

5

THE APPROACH to Red Wind Terrace appeared the same as it had the previous time Horc had entered the Orc city, but like Tragiczan, it was oddly quiet. There were no other players running and jumping around. The vendors were all silent unless approached. The terraced canyon city was still breathtaking in its rugged beauty but didn't have the same impact without sounds beyond what the party was making with their footfalls and idle chatter.

"Anyone have an idea where to find the guild master?" Horc asked as they cleared the bottleneck at the mouth of the canyon.

"Yeah," Tufkakes said rushing up to the front of their party. "When I was here before, one of the silly quests I had to do was finding a list of people to give them notes. One of the people I had to find was a guild master."

Horc grinned, it was nice for something to go smoothly. "Good. Then you get to lead us there." Horc waved her to the front of the party.

"No problem." Tufkakes bounced a bit as he started down the lane.

The predominant colors of the city were reds and oranges, and the majority of the building materials seemed to be either rock or mud, reminding Horc of Santa Fe and Taos where he enjoyed vacationing when he could afford it. Like with Tragiczan, the odd silence just felt wrong. With all the NPCs minding their shops, and moving mutely around the streets with various wares, it was more than a little surreal.

"Hi Ho, Hi Ho," Shortsmyte, a Dwarven Ranger, began to sing.

"What are you doing?" Baladara whirled on him.

Shortsmyte fell quiet, then shrugged. "I don't know about the rest of you, but this quiet is getting to me. If the AI is trying for psychological warfare, it's doing a good job. Tragiczan was bad enough, but there are too many NPCs here. It shouldn't be this quiet. Even when I was playing regular video games on my computer, I never played with the sound off. I was trying to break up the quiet."

Horc nodded. "Actually that makes a lot of sense." He didn't want to let anyone else know how the strangely quiet city was getting to him to. Maybe singing while they walked might make things a little easier.

"We're here," Tufkakes announced, stopping in front of a squat shop that had a sign above it indicating it was Guild HQ.

Horc frowned. "Sounds rather modern for a fantasy game."

Rambull shrugged. "Hey, not everyone's great with names."

"Don't we know it," Theodore spoke up. "At least we don't have to guess at what it is."

"Right." Horc glanced from Tufkakes to Baladara. "Alright, you two, you spent a good part of the hike here chatting, did you come up with a name for us?"

Baladara grinned at Tufkakes. "Okay. I want you to know this wasn't easy. We included Lisa in on some of it, 'cause you know she's awesome with design stuff and all."

"There were a lot of options to be had," Tufkakes agreed. "Some of them, like Horc's Destroyers, we discarded quickly. You're not that big of a barbarian, even if Titanya used to be one."

"And there's nothing wrong with being a Barbarian," Titanya spoke up. "Some of my best friends are Barbars."

"And some of ours too," Baladara replied. "But anyway-"

Horc sighed. "We don't have all day, just get on with it."

Baladara put her hands on her hips and stared at Horc. "And that attitude is why you'll never make it out of middle management."

"The First Responders," Tufkakes said.

"What?" Horc stared at her. "We aren't firemen, or policemen. We're just gamers." The name didn't strike him as fitting. He had a lot of respect for the civil servants he encountered and the name felt somewhat wrong.

Tufkakes shook her head, making her black furry ears wave back and forth. "Wrong. We talked about this, even bounced it past a few of the others, and they're cool with it."

A chorus of "Right" and "Yeah" rang out.

"We're the rescue squad here," Baladara continued. "Nobody else is going to come into this game and save Slasher and the others. Their fate is in our hands. In Halfworld, we are the ones putting out the AI's fire."

"I like it," Bigdaddybear said, patting Horc on the shoulder. "And they do have a point. Look at it this way, ever since Steelmaiden and Slasher got taken by the pirates, your thing has been saving people. Our party started out to keep you alive, and now you're returning the favor. If anyone in this game has the true spirit of a first responder, it's you."

Titanya patted his other shoulder. "And don't think any of us are about to forget what you're doing for us. You're awesome Horc."

A lump formed in Horc's throat. He wasn't used to people looking up to him the way the party was. He was just a simple lead in tech support for Total Immersion Systems. In the game, like in real life, he was just trying to do what was right. The people gathered around him were acting like he was a hero or something.

"Thanks." He swallowed back the lump.

Tufkakes ruffled Horc's hair with a hand that was as much paw as hand. "Good. Now let's get in there and set up this guild so we can all sign the charter and get on with this game."

He turned and walked into the small shop, that turned out to be too small for everyone to get into, so Horc and three others at a time made it up to the Guild Master who stood behind a counter full of papers.

"Hello," Horc said.

The short Orc in bright stylish leathers jumped slightly as he suddenly focused on Horc. He looked like he was ready for a night in a disco rather than helping players organize groups. "How can I help you?"

"We'd like to form a guild," Horc said.

"Fabulous." The Orc's name, in yellow text, read **Harvey Unionman, Orc, Cleric, Level 50**. "I just need a few papers filled out. This requires five people to sign the initial guild charter, and you'll have to stop by the bank with it and open an account there. If you want, you can also design a guild logo to put on your guild tabards, and all Warriors, and Paladins will be able to get the logo on their shields."

There was more to think about than Horc had planned. But, if they were just going to rescue people and then the game would reset, would any of it be things they needed to worry about?

"Right now we just have a name," Horc said as he accepted the papers.

"A name is a good place to start." Harvey pointed to a spot on the top of the first paper. "Right there. You can add the rest any time at any of the other Guild HQs. We have offices in all the major cities, or you can send me mail and I'll get back to you with more forms."

Forms felt like work. Horc picked up a long black quill from the corner of the counter and set to work filling out the first page.

"This'll be fun," Baladara said. "We can design logo, tabards and shields. I might actually roll up a fighter of some sort if we got cool customer shields."

"I've done a bit of graphic arts," Tufkakes added. "We'll make sure it looks awesome."

Horc put his own name down as Guild Head, then listed Baladara, Titanya, Bigdaddybear, and Tufkakes as guild officers. He started to add Slasher, since he was part of the original party, but he wasn't sure if doing something like that might alert the AI to what they were doing, if the AI didn't already know by them interacting with Harvey.

"Sounds like you've got a good crew here," Harvey said. "Every guild needs a good crew, particularly if they're going to survive."

A chill went through Horc and he stared at Harvey. There wasn't any sign on his face that said he was anything more than just the NPC in charge of a small shop, but something in the way he'd said "going to survive" made Horc wonder if the AI was going to manipulate everything in the game to make their quest next to impossible.

Tufkakes, Baladara, and Bigdaddybear put their signatures on the guild charter.

"Let's go out and let three more come in," Bigdaddybear said, waving toward the door.

Horc stood there with the charter as three more came in and added their signatures to the charter. After five people had signed, Horc had to turn to the next page to get the rest of the signatures. When Rambull, the last one, signed the charter, Horc slid the papers back to Harvey.

"Other than stopping by the bank, is there anything else we need to do right now, while we're in town?"

Harvey glanced at the papers, reading over them several times. "Looks like you've got a very powerful guild here, Horc007, Half Orc Ranger. That's good. You're going to need it." Harvey picked up a different quill and made an official flourish at the bottom of the last piece of paper. "Now, once you get a logo figured out, please let me know. You'll only be able to purchase your guild-specific equipment from a Guild HQ office, open in any of the major cities, or order through the mail by sending me a message."

"Thanks." Horc gestured for Rambull to follow him out of the office. He still felt strange about the way Harvey acted. Sometimes it felt like he was working off a script, and sometimes it was like he was either warning, or threatening, Horc couldn't decide which.

Horc breathed a little easier as he stepped out into the bright sunshine and fresh air. He hadn't realized how stuffy it was in the guild office until he was free of it.

"Okay, let's stop by the bank real quick," Horc said, then chuckled. "Not sure we really need to since none of the recent mobs are doing drops."

Baladara laughed. "Who knows, maybe we can get a huge deposit after this adventure is over. I wonder how much gold the AI is worth."

"More than you've got in your account," Tufkakes replied.

Remembering the way from his own wandering quest in Red Wind Terrace, Horc led the way to the bank. Setting up the guild bank account made First Responders even more real. IRL, Horc had never set up any kind of business or joint bank account. He just had the one account for him. He thought it was weird to have more in a game than he had IRL.

The bank was larger than Guild HQ had been, so the entire group was able to fill the space while Horc got it opened and got everyone able to access the account. At Baladara's prompting, he added a daily withdraw limit for everyone but the officers.

"Ah, guys, there's something happening," Jamica called from the back of the group.

"What?" Baladara turned as Horc slipped the paper back to the head banker, the only one who'd responded to them.

As the banker took the paper, the two other bankers behind the bars of the counter came over to him and glared at Horc through the iron bars.

"Ah geez. Guys, I think I've seen this movie, but the zombies looked a little deader." Tufkakes pulled daggers and jumped up on the counter.

Horc spun and looked toward the opening that served as the door, since there didn't appear to be any actual doors in the place. NPCs jammed the opening. They all had various weapons out and looked like they were ready to end the First Responders before they really got a chance to complete their first official adventure as a guild.

6

AS HORC reached for his bow strung over his shoulder, a hand closed over his wrist and yanked him backward.

"No you don't." Tufkakes slashed at the banker's arm, severing the hand from the body.

Horc stumbled against the bank counter, but managed to get his bow unslung and an arrow nocked. The NPC townspeople were turning against them. He didn't know how many people there were in Red Wind Terrace, but he had to get his guild out of the town as fast as possible.

Baladara was already casting a spell, her hands glowing red as she stared toward the opening leading out into the lane. "Everyone hit them as hard as we can."

"Get away from the counter." Tufkakes said as he jumped off the counter. The iron bars that were effective at protecting the bankers, worked both ways as the two uninjured clerks pulled their swords and started stabbing through the bars.

Several spells went off at once, blowing holes through the NPCs trying to get to them. Horc fired arrows as fast as he could, hoping to bring down an adequate number of opponents to let them get out of the bank.

For several minutes, spells, arrows, and daggers flew as they fought to clear the doorway sufficiently to get out. The NPCs were hard to bring down. They all seemed determined to keep the guild in the bank.

"Press forward," Rambull shouted. "I'm using my Charge attack. It'll be five minutes before I can do it again, but I should leave them stunned long enough for us to make it out."

The guild formed around the big Minotauren as he lowered his head. His long horns looked even more dangerous as they spread out to the sides of his skull. Then Rambull bellowed. Magic glistened in a gray glow around him and he Charged.

His horns were almost too wide to clear the opening and one of them scraped orange dirt off the side of it as he went through like an armored bovine freight train. NPCs went down under his hooves or fell back against the wall. None of them moved as the rest of the guild dashed along behind him. Rambull made it halfway across the main square, stunning and stomping NPCs as he went. Then the gray glow around him faded.

Rambull paused, his breath heaving.

"Cover him!" Horc shouted, running as fast as he could to get between Rambull and the NPCs who'd managed to avoid his Charge.

A Fireball shot past him, hitting several NPCs hard, flinging them back into a building across the square.

"I like this upgrade stuff," Baladara said. "Didn't have area of effect spells before."

"It *is* nice," Bigdaddybear agreed as a brown wind howled around them, blowing NPCs out of the way.

"And why didn't you use those earlier?" Horc asked as he got off multiple arrows in a single shot.

"Some things only work outside," Bigdaddybear said as his paws glowed with his next spell.

"Let's get out of the city," Tufkakes shouted from the left.

Horc took a big guard out with a Fire arrow. A notification of loss of reputation with the Orcs flashed on his screen. They weren't getting XP or loot, but their reputation was being impacted by attacking guards… the AI was definitely not playing fair.

"Everyone follow Tufkakes." Horc put a hand on Rambull's shoulder. "You ready to move?"

Rambull let out a long heavy breath. "Don't really have a choice now, do I?"

Horc shook his head. "Not really. I can help if you need it."

"No." Rambull shook his head. "The nice guy thing is why people follow you, Horc. Don't lose it." His hands glowed blue and seconds later a wave of water erupted from where they stood and washed the townsfolks out of their path.

"Thanks." Horc stayed by the big Shaman's side as the guild splashed through the wave's watery wake. The opposition was limited, and the guild members were doing their best to not kill any of the NPCs as they fled the city. It went pretty well until they reached the bottleneck that led to the desert beyond the canyon. Five guards in full armor with huge swords stood there, waiting for the guild to reach them.

Titanya charged to the front of the group. "Tanks, form on me, everyone else stand back and hit them with everything you've got."

Horc readied arrows. He held his multi shots that would've hit several targets, focusing on the guard on the far left. They only had three tanks. Titanya and the two others raced down the center of the bottleneck. With their unwieldy swords swinging easily, they slammed into the three guards at the center. Horc unleashed his arrow with a Flame spell on it as the casters' spells zipped through the air between the guild and the guards.

Rambull stood near the center of the guild chanting a spell that spread out over the party. Horc's next arrow seemed to hit with more force. It knocked more of the guard's health down, but he still didn't get a critical hit. He'd looked at the stats while waiting for Rick to get everything ready so he could log back in. With his level increase, his chance to crit was really high, especially when he fired slowly, focusing each hit.

One of the guards in the center went down. Titanya shouted a war cry, and the other tanks answered.

"We've got incoming from behind," Baladara shouted as she spun at Horc's side. "Guess it's time to see how this new Flame Wall spell works."

"Hurry up guys, we've got to get through this." Horc launched another arrow, this time choosing one of his impact arrows and adding a Poison spell to it. The guard flew backward when the arrow struck him in the chest. He slammed into the side of the bottleneck and his health dropped below a half.

"That should've been a crit," Horc muttered.

The guard's health dropped into the red even as Horc sent his next arrow. Jamica appeared out of the shadows with a bloody dagger in her hand. Horc's arrow put the guard down. He tapped his hair with his bow as a salute as the Troll Rogue disappeared into the shadows again.

With the guild working together, six guards didn't stand a chance, even as their reputation with the Orc faction started sliding toward the negative. Horc told himself that it didn't matter. The odds were that after they defeated the AI and freed everyone, the servers would be reset and they'd have to start over anyway. Everything they'd done would be erased.

"Need a bit of help back here," Baladara said.

Horc turned. A large wall of townspeople were heading their way. It spread across the far end of the bottleneck. They were throwing themselves into the flaming wall that separated them from the First Responders.

"Let me," Scarletcrest, a Gnome Witch with wild vivid red hair and a huge nose for such a little guy, stepped up beside Baladara. "My specialty is ice, but if I can get it far enough from your fire, it should help." He pulled something out of his pouch, muttered something over his hand and as soon as his hand started to glow white, threw it with all his might.

The glowing ball soared over Baladara's Flame Wall, and struck the ground a short distance away from it, landing in the midst of the NPCs. Seconds later the white glow spread out and created a massive barrier of ice, plugging the end of the bottleneck.

"That's great and all," Baladara said. "But there's still a couple dozen between our walls."

"Two more to go here," Bigdaddybear hollered.

"So you don't have long to hold our rear." Horc turned back to the tanks taking down the guards. He loosed an impact arrow with Fire on it at the one closest to Titanya. It caught the guard in the chest, knocking him off his feet. Titanya and Rambull slammed it to the ground. Its health bar flashed red and it disappeared.

Tufkakes and Jamica flashed into sight as the final guard who had been holding off the other two tanks straightened, screamed and fell to the ground. He pixelated in seconds.

"Okay folks, run!" Horc readied another arrow and dashed for the opening the tanks and Rogues had just created.

"Right behind you," Baladara replied. "Come on little guy, we're outta here."

Horc didn't need to turn around to know she was talking to Scarletcrest. He was the only Gnome in the guild, and the only one of them shorter than Baladara.

The bright desert awaited them as they rushed through the open end of the bottleneck. Titanya and Rambull stood with the other tanks. Rambull was casting healing on them.

When Stanoran joined them, he finished healing Titanya, then sighed. "Okay, are we safe enough here to pause and replenish our mana?"

Not knowing how long Scarletcrest's ice wall would stand, Horc shook his head. "Sorry, we need to keep moving." He pointed to his left. "Let's head east until we can't see the edge of the canyon, then we'll head north."

"So that's the direction we need to go?" Stanoran asked.

Horc shrugged and started walking east. "Not exactly sure. We haven't heard back from Rick, have we?" He glanced over his shoulder at the guild members following along behind him until he spotted Bigdaddybear on his right.

"Not yet," Bigdaddybear replied. "Let's get somewhere safe and I'll send him a message. This game needs voice chat with the outside world. That would make this easier."

"Not going to hear me complain about making communications easier." Horc turned his attention to the white sand dunes in front of him. He hadn't expected the NPCs to turn on them like that. The village folk in Tragiczan had been stuck in something similar to a stunned state, except when asked questions. He'd been hoping the other NPCs they encountered would do the same. With the NPCs becoming hostile, the group was in a bit of a pickle. They'd have to rely on their environment for nourishment. They wouldn't be able to stop at an inn or food vendor to get food and drink for healing and mana replenishment.

IT WAS fifteen minutes later when Horc decided they were probably safe to stop. None of the townsfolk had pursued them past the canyon walls, and so far, they hadn't encountered any scorpions, sand worms, or other monsters in the desert. "Okay. Let's pause for a little while." Horc held up his hand for them to halt.

Around him, his guild members dropped to the sands. Several of them lay back and closed their eyes. It was obvious that everyone was beat. Not the most auspicious start to their quest.

"Give me a couple of minutes and I'll check with Rick on how they're coming about locating the AI and the hostages," Bigdaddybear said.

"Sure. Let's hope that they aren't on an island or somewhere we can't get to by walking," Horc said, a gut wrenching realization coming on him. "I doubt we'll be able to ride on boats, blimps, or anything like that without having to fight our way for control."

Baladara smacked her forehead. "Man, I hadn't thought about that. We're up shit creek, aren't we?"

"Maybe not," Rambull said. "If the designers are working on things for us, they might be able to slip something in that could give us a chance."

"Unless it's like a large helicopter, it might not be enough," Stanoran muttered. "I don't know about the other casters, but I was hoping to stock up on water, juice and other beverages to help regain mana. Hostile NPCs might make that impossible."

"The water in the creek outside Steel Helm City was good for that," Horc said, thoughtfully. "Any chance we can rely on our environment for that?"

Baladara chuckled. "In some ways you're still such a newb, but it's not a bad idea. If we can find water. We are in a desert after all."

"But we won't be forever," Horc said. "How about you other casters, anyone have a decent supply of water?"

Scarletcrest raised his hand. "I stocked up before we went to the arena. Still got most of it. I can share."

Horc beamed at the Gnome. "That's the spirit. We can support each other until we find supplies."

Bigdaddybear frowned and opened his eyes. "Okay, good news and bad news. They found the dragon and a concentration of hostages. But they've split the hostages up so we're not going to know who is where."

Several people grumbled at the news.

"The dragon is also on a landmass called Beyond North," he continued. "It's going to be tough to get there. Rick and the others are working on that right now. He says there's an oasis not far from here where we can refill our water containers. He's also got some transport arranged for us here. He'd drop the transport right in front of us, but he can't get a firm lock on our locale until we reach the oasis, since it's a firm location on the map."

"Transport will be good," Horc said. If it was something where they weren't going to have to hike across the continent, it would be a good thing. With the game being weird on them, Horc wondered what kind of transport Rick was going to be able to arrange.

7

FOLLOWING RICK'S directions on how to find the oasis, it was less than an hour's walk from where they had collapsed. Massive palm trees jutted out of the white sands and a large pond, not exactly large enough to be a lake, occupied the middle of the grove. Tied to several of the palm trees were ten massive lizards, or at least that how Horc saw them until he saw the text over their scaly heads. They were a variety of blue, green, purple and red and the size of cows if he didn't include the tail which was as long as the bodies were and in constant motion. The green text over their heads read **Stonzard, level forty-nine mount**.

"Yeah, these look like fun," Baladara muttered as she walked up to one. "Have I ever told anyone that I'm really not into horses?"

Horc laughed and wasn't going to add that he wasn't either. "Then it's a good thing these aren't horses." Each of the huge lizards had saddles already on them, and the saddlebags bulged with what Horc hoped were supplies.

"Yes!" Stanoran shouted as he opened the saddlebags one of the purple lizards. "Water and food. Bigdaddybear, make sure to tell your husband thanks for us."

Bigdaddybear grinned as he checked the bags on one of the green ones. "Will do. I figured he could come up with something helpful."

Horc walked over to the lone red lizard. It had bright red streaks running from its head back to its haunches. Overall, its hide was a fairly deep brick red and its eyes were a bright yellow. It was the only one of the group that wasn't constantly lashing its tail, and Horc hoped that meant it had a calmer demeanor than the others. He checked his bags, and like the others found food, water, and a few odd sparkling crystals. Pulling out one of the crystals, he held it up to the bright sun.

Crystal of Magical Enhancement.

"Anybody know what these crystals are?" He turned to the rest of the group and held up the clear crystal.

Scarletcrest, who was already on his purple lizard stood in the saddle and raised one of his own. "They're special items to increase spell power. I've been looking for some since someone posted about them in the game wiki. They're fairly rare, and only last a few minutes. I guess that's why we've got so many of them."

"Another way Rick's trying to help," Bigdaddybear said, swinging into his own saddle. Being a huge Ursan, sitting on the lizard didn't look as odd as it might have if Rick had sent horses to them.

"How do we use them?" Horc slipped his back into the saddlebag and put his foot in the stirrup to mount his lizard.

"You crush them in your hand to release the magic," Scarletcrest said.

"Sounds fairly easy," Baladara replied. She shook her lizard's reins and then looked confused when it didn't start forward. "Okay folks, there's no gear shift here, how do I put it in drive?"

Tufkakes laughed. "Heels to the side." He pulled his green lizard next to Baladara. "It would help if you put your heels down and toes up."

Baladara's lizard snapped at Tufkakes'. Tufkakes' snapped back, then lashed out with its tail.

"Stop that you stupid things," Baladara complained as she clung to the saddle and dropped the reins. "This isn't going to be a lot of fun, is it?"

BEYOND THE BOSS

Theodore sighed as he started his mount forward. "This whole game stopped being fun when the AI decided it could try to kill us."

"There is that," Horc agreed, although he didn't want to admit that he was having a lot more fun in Halfworld than he'd had in any fantasy game before, and it was enough that if it hadn't been for the AI, he might give up on Galactic Explorers, the scifi mmorpg he normally played. Being in the middle of a rescue mission wasn't the time to announce how much fun he was having. It was even great running with the rest of the players in the guild. In the other games he played, he normally ran solo, and when he needed extra manpower, he'd hire henchmen, or crew for his ship, but always NPCs. Not that hiring NPCs in Halfworld would be safe while the AI was trying to kill them. But, NPCs wouldn't be having the problems Baladara was getting her mount to go. They wouldn't have the snarky conversations players did, either. Overall, it was refreshing, in a life and death sort of way.

With a bit more prompting from the others, Baladara managed to get her mount going and they continued across the desert, heading north out of the oasis.

After a while, the gentle rocking motion of the lizard, and the blandness of the undulating white landscape made Horc drowsy. He crossed his arms, keeping a light hold on the reins and not realizing how tired he was, even as his head dropped toward his chest.

"HORC! EVERYONE, we've got a problem." Bigdaddybear's voice tore through Horc's sleep.

Jerking erect, Horc yanked on his lizard's reins and nearly lost his balance. For a second the white sand beneath the lizard flashed in his vision, then he grabbed hold of the saddle horn and righted himself. He shook his head and rubbed his eyes. "What's wrong?"

Bigdaddybear was riding right next to Horc. "Look." He pointed to the north.

The blue sky had vanished and a huge white wave looked like it was about to crash over them.

Horc pulled on the reins, bringing his mount to a stop. "Is that a sand storm?"

"Sure looks like it." Bigdaddybear replied. "And it looks like it's heading right at us."

"We could circle the lizards before it gets here," Titanya suggested. "If we can get them to lie down and form a scaly wall, it might help block the worst of it."

"Or we could try some magic and keep riding," Bigdaddybear suggested. "I have a couple of spells that might help us."

"Not a bad idea," Baladara agreed. "A big shield spell cast over the group might block enough of the sand and wind to let us keep going."

"But how would we know where we're going?" Horc asked, not liking the idea of riding blind across the desert. They'd been lucky since leaving Red Wind Terrace and hadn't run into any desert-dwelling monsters, but he figured that could change at any moment, and if Baladara, one of their big hitters, was caught up in casting their protection they might be in trouble, especially if they just stumbled on a nest of scorpions, or snakes.

"I can help with that," Scarletcrest announced. "I can cast a vision spell and focus it a little beyond her shield spell. It would be like trying to drive using a camera for guidance, awkward, but possible."

"I like the idea," Tufkakes said. "Keeps us moving."

Although he was still worried about not being prepared for something in the middle of the storm, Horc nodded. "Okay. Everyone stay sharp. Baladara, use one of those crystals to give you a bit of extra oomph. Scarletcrest get your spell ready for when the storm hits us. Let's tighten things up as much as these lizards will let us." Horc stayed at the front of the group, as Baladara and Scarletcrest took up positions on either side of him.

When the first grains of sand began hitting them, Baladara started her spell. Her hands glowed yellow for a moment, then the wind and sand stopped. She let out a contented sigh and seemed to relax in her saddle. "Nice to see this works. I'm going to have to recast every three minutes, which might get to be a pain after a while."

"Which is why you've got friends," Tufkakes said sounding more cheerful than Horc felt at that moment.

The wall of white enveloped Baladara's protective sphere. IRL Horc had never seen a white sandstorm. They were normally black or dirty brown. The storm in the Scalteon Desert looked more like a snowstorm as the pale grains of sand pelted the magical shield blocking out the damaging wind and sand. It was like being in the middle of a snow globe, but the flakes and spinning were on the outside, not the inside.

"Wow, even with magical sight, it's hard to see out there." Scarletcrest shook his head as if to clear his vision. "Everything's moving so fast and furiously."

"Do you want me to try to generate some wind blowing the opposite direction and see if that clears things in front of us?" Bigdaddybear offered.

Horc shook his head. "No. I don't want all our casters caught up in this. If something happens I want at least one of you to be fresh and ready to fight."

"Renewing spell," Baladara announced. "I don't know if there'll be a moment of storm or not." Her hands glowed as she began casting the spell.

It didn't feel like it had been three minutes since she did the first spell, but Horc had always been horrible at the game so many corporate trainers liked to play to have phone techs judge a minute of silence to put them in the shoes of customers who were on hold.

A gust of wind laden with dust lashed at them, then cut off as Baladara finished her spell.

"Good job," Horc said.

"Ah guys, I think we've got a problem," Scarletcrest muttered.

Horc's heart sank. They'd just entered the storm, it wasn't a good time for trouble to find them. If something happened to Baladara they'd be at the storm's mercy. "What's wrong?"

Scarletcrest pointed up and to the front of them. "Dragons."

"Dragons? As in plural?" Horc inwardly cursed the sandstorm. He couldn't see anything past the invisible magical shield protecting them from the winds and sand.

"Shit." Baladara screamed as claws and a scaly body hit the shield above them. She rocked in her saddle and her lizard skittered to the side.

"Oh no you don't." Bigdaddybear reached out and grabbed the lizard's reins. "I need you to calm down." His hands glowed a light blue and after a second, the glow traveled across to the lizard.

For the first time since they'd left the oasis, the big beast looked sleepy as its green eyelids drooped slightly.

Another heavily scaled body slammed into the shield and Baladara grabbed her head. "Guys, they aren't getting through, but I don't know how much of this I can take."

"And you'll have to renew the shield in about two minutes," Rambull said. "I've got an idea, but we need to stop for a bit."

"There's four dragons that I can see," Scarletcrest said.

"I can't keep that many out," Baladara moaned.

"Maybe you don't have to." Rambull glanced at Theodore and Bigdaddybear. "Let's knock this storm back on its ass, then take out these dragons. Wind spells as the shield drops."

Horc liked where his thinking was going. He pulled out his bow and nocked an arrow. "Tanks and Rogues, get ready, we're about to have dragons."

8

EVERYTHING SEEMED to happen at once. The winds for the spells erupted out of Baladara's shield. Dragons dropped out of the skies around the party. Battle cries rang out, and Horc loosed a series of Fire Arrows into the dragons as Baladara screamed at the top of her lungs.

Horc's red lizard charged toward the parting of the storm, as Horc tried to get another round of arrows off. The Dragons were getting their footing and chasing some of the other lizards and party members. Those members of the party, like Titanya and Stanoran, who'd gotten off their mounts were faring better than the ones who'd opted to stay astride as the lizards scattered in all directions.

Pulling on his mount's reins, Horc tried to turn the beast around. His party was in trouble and needed him. The lizard jerked back, hissing. As the party shouted and cursed behind him, Horc fought to get control of the lizard. It reared up hissing and pawing the air. Horc forced its head around, wishing Bigdaddybear was there to calm it like he had Baladara's steed.

Lightning danced in the sandstorm as the opening created by the winds began to close.

Somehow, Horc managed to get his lizard pointed back toward the party. From what he could see, several people were missing, and there were only three Dragons, not four. Titanya and Stanoran were pounding on one, a small Dragon, at least by Horc's recollection, that had blue scales and a black frilled ruff. They were doing pretty good at holding it off Baladara who rolled on the ground holding her head, continuing to scream.

Horc got off an impact Fire arrow, then pulled on his lizard's reins to bring the freaking thing to a shaky stop. His best bet was to stay back and fire arrows, letting his tanks do their job of close combat.

Rambull glowed with a strange red magic as he grabbed hold of a slightly larger Dragon. He gripped it by the horns and went to flip it over like he was a cowboy bulldogging a calf.

Switching targets for a few quick shots, Horc sent arrows into Rambull's Dragon. Its health flashed with each strike. Then Bigdaddybear jumped on the beast and whacked it hard on the head. The Dragon faltered and fell over with the combined efforts of Bigdaddybear and Rambull.

Horc got more arrows in the one Titanya and Stanoran were fighting, helping drop it to under half. He wondered where Tufkakes, Jamica, and Scarletcrest were.

The fourth Dragon reappeared, charging out of the sandstorm with Tufkakes and Jamica on it, hitting hard and fast with daggers. Horc got a Poisoned razor arrow into it before it disappeared into the storm on the other side of the fight. The wind and sand from the failing splitting of the storm began to hit Horc in the back.

Somewhere in the storm a Dragon screamed, at least he thought it was a Dragon and not one of the lizard mounts. Horc hit the Dragon Theodore was astride. The Ursan was holding onto its wings like he was trying to use them to steer the monster. The Dragon kept bending its neck around, trying to snap at Theodore. Horc hit it in the head twice with impact arrows. The Dragon stumbled and turned toward Horc.

The Dragon spun, not seeming to care about the Ursan Shaman holding onto its wings. It appeared hell bent on hitting Horc. Getting a couple more arrows into it only dropped the thing to three quarters. More than ever, Horc wished they were still able to do critical hits, he had no idea how long they were going to have to pound on each Dragon to bring them down, let alone all four of them. With his next arrow, the winds were whipping around him and blew it to the side just as his lizard reared again and took off into the storm.

"Damn it." Horc jumped from the lizard. He didn't have time to fight his mount, the storm and the Dragon. The landing hurt his knees, and jarred his bow out of his hand.

The sandstorm engulfed him just as he pulled his halberd and braced it spear-like for the Dragon's charge, hoping the beast wouldn't come in at an angle and miss the spear tip, getting Theodore hit instead.

His luck improved and the Dragon hit the tip of the halberd. The axe blade stopped the beast from sliding too far on the weapon, but it was enough to drop the thing down to half.

"Wahoo!" Theodore shouted, then ran along the dragon's back to drive a short sword into the thing's head. The blow knocked an eighth of the thing's health back.

The Dragon jerked back, pulling itself free of Horc's halberd, and nearly yanking the weapon out of his grip. It shook its head furiously and opened its jaws. Lightning danced out of its maw. Horc threw himself on the ground, rolling out of the way as bolts of electricity lashed the sands. The elemental fury struck Theodore and every hair on his body stood out as he flew off the Dragon's neck.

The sandstorm made it hard to tell exactly, but it looked like his sword went flying out of his hand as Theodore was flung from the Dragon.

Horc slashed with the halberd's axe blade catching the Dragon in the throat. Shocking power raced across his weapon, jumping from the metal blade across the decorative iron bands on the handle and hit Horc for lots of damage. The impact of the electricity threw him backward into the sandstorm, knocking out nearly half of his health in the one harsh exchange.

The sandstorm closed around him. The winds muffled the sounds of the other fights going on near him. The sands hit his exposed skin, stinging at first and quickly turning to burning. Horc reached into his boot and pulled out a dagger. It wouldn't do much against a dragon, but unless he happened to stumble across either his bow or his halberd, it was all he had, other than arrows that he could stab something with as well.

Grabbing the edge of his cloak, Horc tore off a long piece of it and wrapped it around his face. That helped block some of the pain, but the storm was hitting so hard that every minute his health dropped a little bit. He wanted to sit down and wait the storm out, but he couldn't abandon his team like that. He held out his hands and stumbled forward into the maelstrom.

Since he couldn't exactly see where he was going, Horc looked at the display showing the guild members. Everyone was still alive, although Baladara was down to under a quarter of her health, and quickly falling. The others had taken damage too, with Bigdaddybear and Stanoran being the two closest to full health, but they were the healers and that made sense.

Something that felt like thin leather brushed Horc's head. A huge shadow fell over him. Reflexively, he slashed out with the dagger. The sharp blade caught something. A loud scream of pain rewarded his efforts. Realizing he'd just cut a Dragon's wing, Horc grabbed blindly, hoping he could catch the leading edge of the wing. Something came down hard on his outstretched arm. Pain shot through him, but he managed to catch hold with the hand not holding the dagger and yanked hard.

Remembering Theodore's inability to break the Dragon's wings, Horc opted for another tactic with the Dragon as he slammed his dagger into the beast's side where the wing joined with the body. The dagger sank deep and warm blood splashed out over Horc's hand, making the dagger hard to hold onto.

Since he was attacking the Dragon, its stat bars showed up on his display. Its health was down into the orange. Then the Dragon screamed again. It lurched to the side, shoving Horc hard. A short sword came through the Dragon's throat, barely missing Horc's head.

"Hey!" Horc shouted as he jumped back.

The Dragon's health bar flashed red, then disappeared. The beast dropped to the ground and pixelated.

Theodore stood on the other side of the vacant space. "Dude, that was intense." His health bar was quickly heading to the orange with each second the storm continued to lash them.

"Yeah, it was." Horc took a deep breath and reached back into his pack, hoping to grab a couple of health potions before the storm killed them. His fingers curled around cool glass vials. He pulled two out and thrust one toward Theodore. "Here, drink this."

As soon as the Ursan Shaman took the vial, Horc uncorked his own and downed it. The taste was as bad as he remembered, a bit like salty fish water. But as the foulness faded from his mouth, his health went back to full. No sooner was he back at full than the damage from the sandstorm continued to pound at him and started gnawing it down bit by bit.

"We've got to find the others," Horc shouted.

"Baladara looks like she's in bad shape." Theodore turned. "I think she's over here."

"How can you tell?" Horc stumbled through the sand that was drifting around his feet even though he'd only been standing still for a minute or so.

"The party map."

"What?" Horc wanted an answer, but something slammed into him from the whiteness of the sandstorm. It was smooth hide, not like the lizards, but like another dragon. He stabbed his dagger into the leathery flesh that hit him. A bone chilling cold hit him hard. He held tight to his dagger, determined not to lose it like he had his halberd and bow.

"Damn!" Theodore shouted from nearby. He hit the Dragon hard with something.

Horc stabbed the Dragon again, doing his best to ignore the cold that radiated out from the Dragon's body. A Fireball came from somewhere in the storm and hit the Dragon in the head.

"Hold him still." Rambull's voice was muffled by the wind, and Horc only hoped the Minotauren Shaman was talking to them.

Horc grabbed hold of the Dragon's head, and Rambull's fingers brushed Horc's arm, letting him know the Ursan was struggling from the other side of the Dragon. Then Rambull charged out of the storm. He had his head down and hit the Dragon with all his might.

"Twist!" Theodore shouted and shoved against Horc's arm as the Dragon staggered back under Rambull's assault.

Hoping he understood correctly, Horc pulled the Dragon's head around as hard as he could. There was a resounding crack and the last bit of the Dragon's health dropped away and it vanished into the digital world that formed it.

"One more," Rambull yelled as he staggered to his feet near Horc.

"Horc, give me a healing potion for Baladara and you help the others finish off the last one." Theodore put his hand out to Horc.

Still not sure how they were seeing the other party members on the map, Horc figured it was Baladara's best hope. He pulled another potion and put it in Theodore's hand.

Rambull headed off into the storm. "Follow me."

Horc rushed to not lose him. The sounds of battle were dying back, but the storm howled on. His own health was back to under three quarters due to the Dragon and the constant damage from the storm.

Something glowed bright in the storm as Horc followed Rambull.

A battle cry rang out over the howl of the winds. Horc kept going toward the cry. His foot caught on something and he fell hard on the ground, getting a mouth full of sand. His health dropped again.

His head spun as he managed to sit and spit, trying to clear the sand from his tongue.

Another battle cry fought the storm for dominance. Horc recognized the sound of Titanya triumphing over something, or someone.

"That should be the last one," Horc muttered, and remembered the party had a chat option. He quickly opened a window.

Can everyone get this? Horc

I can. Baladara

I think we've got them down. I can account for three. Horc

We can account for two. Bigdaddybear

And if you were helping Titanya bring down the last one, it's one of the ones I'm counting, so that makes four. Horc

Sounds right. Titanya

Then everyone come together on me. If anyone still has a mount bring it. I think it's time to circle the lizards. Horc

We'll be there in a couple of minutes. Baladara

Maybe you can get that shield up again. Tufkakes

We'd like to get out of this storm. Jamica

Nope. We're just going to sit tight and drink healing potions. Horc

Might be the best option. If we need to, we can cast healing on folks as we take damage. Stanoran

It wasn't the best plan Horc had ever heard, but it was a plan. They wouldn't be stumbling into anything in the storm, and he just hoped the AI wouldn't send anything else to hit them until after it was over. As the others gathered around, they sat in a tight circle, putting Baladara and Scarletcrest in the center to protect their smallest from the worst of the storm if they could. He also hoped it would give the casters a chance to help defend if something went bad before they could all see beyond the storm. Once everyone was circled and they spread their cloaks out wide, most of the damage from the storm was buffeted, and their health wasn't taking constant hits. It gave Horc the hope they'd survive if the storm moved on like a storm in the real world.

9

HORC DUG through another pile of sand, hoping to uncover one of his dropped weapons. The sandstorm had blown itself out after several hours.

"What did you guys do to Mikey?" Baladara's voice raised in irritation. She'd been curled up in the middle of everyone during the storm and hadn't moved since. Her health was back to normal, and everyone had just assumed she'd gone AFK for a while and hadn't been too worried about it.

Horc hurried from the pile of sand to where Baladara, obviously being driven by Lisa, stood with her hands on her hips glaring at all of them. "What do you mean? Is something wrong with him?" Since Mike and Lisa were using VR goggles and gloves, they shouldn't be at risk of game feedback like the pod users were. He'd have hated it if something happened to Mike, but the AI was figuring out how to kill players IRL.

"He's a drooling gibbering mess. Honestly, it's not an uncommon state for him, but normally I'm the one who leaves him that way." She pursed her lips, then her face softened. "I managed to get him into bed, and he finally relaxed enough and went to sleep."

"Good." Horc relaxed a bit. "She… ah he was trying to hold a magical shield against a sand storm when Dragons attacked. I think there was some magical feedback."

"But you guys aren't using pods, he shouldn't have gotten that bad a feedback." Bigdaddybear came over, leading two of lizards by their reins.

"I don't think we totally know the rules at the moment," Tufkakes said. "The AI is acting up pretty badly."

"You're right there," Baladara said. "If we're the only ones using basic VR, maybe the AI's using us as guinea pigs for something."

Horc shook his head, then pinched his nose. "I don't like this. What if the AI finds a way to permanently hurt you? You've got kids."

"I don't think that's going to happen," Baladara replied. "There's only so much damage a game can give someone who's not in a pod. We'll be fine."

"If you want to log out, we're not going to think any less of you guys." Horc frowned and had the urge to pace. He managed to push the urge down and put his hands behind his back.

"We're sticking here until everyone's out," Baladara said. "We've been through this mess this long, we're here for you."

"Thanks, Lisa." Bigdaddybear walked over and gave her a huge hug. Tufkakes and the rest of the guild walked up and joined the embrace.

As Horc put his arms around the others, he felt a little silly at first, but there was something right and comforting about it as they stood there. Sure, he only knew Mike, Lisa, and Stan IRL, but the rest were quickly becoming friends and family. He couldn't wait to get out of the game and meet David, Rick, Shelia and the rest. They were forming bonds in the game that he had no doubt were going to continue once they were all free of it.

HORC LET out a long sigh and stared at the swath of desert they'd spent hours going over, trying to find everything they'd lost in the storm. They'd gotten lucky and the lizards hadn't wandered very far. The huge mounts had hunkered down a few hundred feet from where they'd started and waited for the wind and sand to stop. Everything that had been in their saddle bags was right there and only a little of the color of the bags had been blasted off by the force of the sand. The lizards had required some Druid healing from Bigdaddybear, since the Priest healing from Stanoran hadn't worked on them.

While digging through the sand, the party had managed to find everything dropped, except for Horc's halberd. He hadn't been real fond of the weapon, but it had been something for when they got into close quarters. None of the rest of the party was carrying spare weapons, so Horc was left with his bow and arrows. He was just going to have to make an effort to stay back from the main part of a fight and shoot arrows at their opponents. That had been working out so well of late he hoped they didn't run into anything his dagger wouldn't prove effective against.

Horc grabbed the reins of his red lizard, then stopped and stared at the beast for a moment. "Look, no more running off, okay. From now on, you're going to act like any good horse and just hang around when shit's going down."

Theodore laughed behind him. "You realize that if these lizards had been horses, they'd have probably run for the hills when the Dragons showed up and would still be running as hard and fast as they could."

"I knew there was a reason I prefer motorized transport." Horc put his foot in the stirrup and swung up on the lizard's back.

"But this is a fantasy game, so unless there's a bit of steam power puttering around here, no motorized transport." Theodore also mounted.

"Some of the Gnomes have steam preferences," Scarletcrest said, as he rode up alongside Horc, still looking small and out of place on the lizard, almost like a human toddler placed on a Clydesdale. "Maybe when the AI problem is dealt with, we can go explore some Gnomish areas and see what we can find."

Having Scarletcrest want to continue playing the game with the guild after the AI was fixed brought a slight smile to Horc. Even after all that had happened to him in Halfworld, he wanted to play more once it was safe to. He hoped the others felt the same way as Scarletcrest. It would be good to keep the guild together, and keep adventuring, especially if it wasn't in a life-or-death situation.

"Hey, we've got a locale!" Bigdaddybear shouted. "Rick's sending us a quest now so we can find it."

Horc turned in his saddle and stared at him. "I thought the AI was interfering with the quests."

Bigdaddybear shrugged. "Rick or one of the other developers must've found a way around that."

A window popped up in Horc's view.

Find the Dragon, free the hostages and free Halfworld

Accept - Decline

Unlike other quests Horc had gotten in the game, there wasn't a list of rewards or anything more than the very basic window. He focused on the accept option. The window blinked and disappeared. The quest icon on the bottom of his field of view flashed and a white arrow appeared on the map in the upper right corner of his vision.

"Now we just follow the arrow," Bigdaddybear said, and got his lizard moving back across the desert.

Having a firm destination helped Horc feel better. Before it had felt like they were just going in a general direction and were all hoping they weren't going to have to turn around and go somewhere else when they got to the Far North.

"Wow, this is going to take a while," Titanya said with a whistle. "Too bad we can't take a flight of some sort."

"And risk the NPCs near the flight path turning on us?" Stanoran asked. He then shook his head. "No thanks. I'd rather spend another day or so riding along than have to fight our way in and out of a flight."

"Rick's got some guys working on getting us a boat or something similar for when we reach the coast," Bigdaddybear said. "He said something about trying to make it fast, but that could mean a lot of things."

"But before we can worry about that, we've got to get to the coast," Rambull said. "I know there's a lot of the map that's not filled in for me, but that's still a long way, through uncharted territory."

Horc pulled up his main map and frowned. He had to zoom out several times to get a clear idea of where they were going, and it was in the center of the frozen continent north of where they were currently riding. From what he could tell by zooming in and out between their currently location and their destination, there were several different zones they were going to have to traverse, much like when they'd battled their way through the Gnoll King's dungeon. He just hoped this adventure was going to be easier than that one was.

"We pass through the Procyan and Ursan starting area," Tufkakes said. "It's nothing hardcore and as long as we don't get completely mobbed, shouldn't be a problem."

Theodore nodded. "Yeah, lower-level small mobs shouldn't slow us down."

Horc sighed, even if they were lower level the last time the two of them had been there, that was before the AI had gone rogue on them, it was entirely possible everything in the zone had been boosted and was just waiting for them to ride through to their deaths. "We'll still want to avoid NPCs when at all possible. No cities. I'm going to rely on you two to keep us out of trouble."

Tufkakes nodded, then gave Horc a quick salute. "Roger that fearless leader. No towns or other centers of activity. The area is mostly forest and mountains. We should be able to go around the areas that lead to the caves where the cities are."

"There might be a slight problem with that," Theodore pursed his lips, making his muzzle scrunch down and look odd, like he'd eaten something that hadn't agreed with him. "The passage through the mountains goes through Winter's Rest. If we don't go through the city, we're going to have to fight our way through the mountain pass that's controlled by the Frozen Yetis."

Horc frowned. "Frozen Yetis? Isn't that repetitive?"

Theodore shrugged. "Game developers never claimed to be great at naming things."

"Geez, men." Titanya banged her sword on her shield. "We'll meet them with our steel out and smash their skulls in if we have to."

"As long as they don't get the drop on us and do the same thing to us," Stanoran said.

"Stan, you were a Pally before you became a Priest, both are tanks, what are you afraid of?" Titanya turned in her saddle and looked back over her shoulder at him.

Stanoran shrugged. "Another scene like back in Red Wind Terrace. Too many NPCs and not enough of us."

"It's a low level area," Scarletcrest said. "We're almost at level cap. We should be fine."

"Yeah, we'll be fine." Horc said, trying to sound more enthusiastic than he felt. Heading into a pass full of Yetis might present a major problem, but he figured it was a safer option than going through a major city in a starting zone that would be full of NPCs of all levels. He just hoped they weren't going to have to battle Yetis in a blizzard. After the struggle of the Dragons and the sandstorm, that wasn't something he wanted to do. They still weren't sure how much of things like tactics the AI understood. Would it know they were going to have to either go through a city or a mountain pass to get to it? Would it take steps to impede their progress? Would it be easier to just find other ways over the mountains?

He doubted the last option would work. Most games he'd ever played, when faced with a landscape feature like mountains, there were normally only a couple of ways, or one way through or over it. They'd just have to deal with the Yetis and hope for the best.

10

HORC SHIVERED and wished he had some winter clothes. After being in the desert, the cold of the high mountain pass was more than he wanted to deal with. However, it was their only way through. To that point, their journey hadn't been too hard, the forest had presented a few minor mobs, mostly low-level monsters the party didn't have trouble dispatching. The majority of them went down with single hits thanks to everyone's levels being significantly above their attackers.

Theodore slipped back through the rocks that bordered the trail going up into the mountains. He looked tired as he walked back to where the party stood at the base of the trail, most standing next to their mounts. He strolled up to Horc and Bigdaddybear. "Okay, here's what we found."

Horc glanced around. "Where's Tufkakes and Jamica?"

"They stayed up there, ready to attack from behind if the Yetis start down toward us. It's an edge we might need."

Horc didn't like splitting the party, but it made sense for the two Rogues to prepare an ambush just in case it was needed. "Sounds good."

"That's what I said when TK suggested it." Theodore took a long breath and wiped his face. "Since we've got about thirty of them up there, that'll help give us a bit of an edge."

Bigdaddybear whistled. "Thirty? That's a fair number of Yetis."

"Right." Theodore nodded. "And there might be more in the caves up there. The thirty was just what we saw. The good thing is they're about level thirty-five. I don't know why. Previously they were about level ten to twelve, but at least they aren't maxed out."

Rambull sighed. "You're right there. Thirty maxed out mobs isn't something we want to take on. Thirty level thirty-fives we might be able to handle."

"We're going to have to stay sharp and be ready for anything," Horc said. The odds were in their favor, but all it would take would be a slip up and the close odds could turn against them. As a party, they had taken down opponents ten levels above them with a bit of a struggle. A mistake on their part could give the Yetis a break.

"A standard battle formation should be enough," Titanya said. "Tanks in front, healers and damage folks behind. That'll also make a good attack plan to make the most of the Rogues in behind the bad guys."

"I agree." Horc still missed having a melee. He wondered if the Yetis would leave anything lying around in their encampment that he might be able to pick up and use. Since their kills weren't lootable, he hoped something would be.

"Okay, that's a good idea and all, here's the thing." Theodore put his hands behind his back and a concerned look crossed his furry face. "There's a couple of Yeti shamans up there with them. They'll probably be doing what they can to keep the others alive. We'll probably want to try to take them out first. They're also level forty."

"Level forties we can deal with," Titanya said. "To be on the safe side, Horc and the casters should target them first. If they try to get past us to them, we can go after them."

Horc nodded. "Okay. Let's do this so we can get through the pass and keep moving. The sooner we reach the shore, the sooner we can see what kind of boat Rick's got ready for us and we can get across the ocean." He started to mount his red lizard, then stopped. "Mounts, or no mounts?"

Theodore looked thoughtful for a moment. "Let's use mounts. The trail is fairly smooth up that way. We can maybe ride a few down if we need to."

Titanya laughed. "I like the way you think."

They mounted and head up the trail.

Since they were riding, Horc felt strange being toward the back of the group. Sure when they had been in the dungeon he'd let Steelmaiden and Slasher lead their charges, but since they'd been on the lizards, he was normally in front leading. The trail started out fairly flat, but quickly sloped upward toward the mountain pass, visible as a low spot between two snow-covered peaks.

About halfway up, they encountered their first couple of Yetis. They jumped out from some large rocks, hitting Titanya and Stanoran hard enough to knock them from their mounts. By the time Horc had his bow unslung and an arrow nocked, they were both dead from caster spells and Titanya's massive sword.

Titanya caught her lizard and remounted. "For the first attack, that wasn't too bad." Her health bar had barely dropped in the brief encounter.

Stanoran frowned at a huge dent in his armor from where he'd fallen to the ground. "Speak for yourself. We can't get armor repairs until we get done with this quest. Chainmail doesn't dent the way plate does."

"So—" Titanya snorted "—get some chainmail."

Stanoran rolled his eyes as he mounted. "And where am I supposed to do that? We aren't getting drops, we can't talk to NPCs without them trying to take our heads off. It's not like Bigdaddybear's husband is going to be able to just leave us armor and weapons lying around." He settled in the saddle and pointed at Horc. "Even our leader doesn't have a weapon because we can't get him one to replace the one the sandstorm ate. We need to get this quest done so we can get this game back to normal."

Nobody said anything more as they resumed riding up the pass. Stanoran had hit the nail on the head and there wasn't anything any of them could add. His words reinforced how hard the game was getting, and how much danger they were all in if things didn't change for the better.

"WE'RE ALMOST there," Theodore said in a low voice as they made it up a particularly steep section of trail, There had been three more Yeti ambushes along their way, none of them very bad, although Stanoran did suffer a couple more dents in his armor.

Horc had been riding with his reins in one hand and his bow at the ready in the other. He nodded and Titanya, Rambull, and Stanoran rode out in front of everyone by a short distance.

Something moved in the boulders along the trail.

"Up there!" Horc pointed with his bow. The movement was in between the tanks and the rest of the party.

"Got it." Bigdaddybear said and a ball of brown Druid magic rolled off his fingertips. Seconds later a huge white shape jumped out from behind the rocks coming toward the casters.

Mage and Witch spells caught it just as Horc's first round of impact arrows hit it. The Yeti rolled backward in midair and vanished, blown to bits by their attack.

Then it was like an avalanche as more of the monsters hurled themselves down the pass at the party.

"Shit!" Baladara began casting Fireballs as fast as she could.

Horc wasn't sure how many of them there were, but he was fairly sure Theodore had been wrong about their numbers.

Firing arrow after arrow, using Multishot as soon as the cooldown finished, Horc did his best to add as much pain as he could to the Yetis that attacked the party. Most of the monsters went down with just a few hits, but some of them were obviously being targeted by healers as their health bars started to drop, then rose again to full health quickly.

"Find the healers," Horc yelled as he finished off one that had been hit by a Fireball Baladara cast.

The Yetis swarmed over the party. Horc kept shooting arrows, wishing he either had a melee weapon or something that would help.

In the distance a deep howl rolled across the mountains, carrying over the sound of battle. Although the Yetis were strangely silent, like all the other NPCs and mobs they'd battled on their way across the continent.

Horc fired another round of arrows and was prepping his next. He selected impact arrows and readied a Multiple Shot spell as a huge dark ball of fur entered the fray. It looked vaguely like Wolf, and when Horc loosed his barrage of arrows, he glanced at his screen. The companion icon that had been missing from his view since he'd returned to the game was there.

The text over the fast moving fury of fang and fur said Wolf, but the thing was easily three times the size of his companion. It savaged one of the Yetis, then threw it up in the air as it vanished in a swirl of pixels. Horc's heart soared as Wolf ran through the Yetis destroying them as he came. Trying to anticipate his companion's path, Horc focused his fire. He'd put a couple of arrows in a Yeti, and Wolf would finish them off.

"Damn, that wolf is good," Theodore said standing near Horc.

Horc grinned. "Yes, he is."

We got one of the shamans. Tufkakes

Thanks. Horc quickly replied as he sent a volley of razor arrows into the closest Yeti.

More Fireballs seared the air between them and the Yetis, then Titanya and Stanoran were there, laying waste to them from behind.

"Help!" Scarletcrest yelped.

Twisting in his saddle, Horc looked back as five Yetis pulled the Gnome Witch from his mount. "No." Horc hit one of them with a Fire impact arrow.

Wolf rushed past Horc without pause. He leapt over Scarletcrest's mount and hit one of the Yetis hard enough to knock it to the ground. Horc sliced the thing deep with a razor arrow and it vanished.

Scarletcrest's health bar was in the orange.

Horc changed targets. As he loosed another arrow, a new Yeti jumped out from the rocks. Its trajectory was perfect to intersect Horc's arrow. The great white beast hit the ground hard, and rolled toward the rocks on the other side of the trail.

"Damn." Horc tried again to target one of the Yetis on Scarletcrest, whose health was down into the red. "Bigdaddybear, can you get to him?" Horc shouted at the top of his lungs.

"Busy right now." Bigdaddybear replied.

Horc fired an arrow off and glanced at the party icons. Scarletcrest's health was nearly depleted. Bigdaddybear's was half down, and his mana was farther down than that. Baladara's mana was in the red. Titanya's health was getting low.

Deciding to ignore the party icons in his field of view, Horc focused on the Yetis pounding on Scarletcrest. He got off two more shots, the first taking down the one he'd shot a couple of times already, the second starting on a new target that Wolf pulled off Scarletcrest and savaged. The final Yeti drove its claws into Scarletcrest and the Gnome blinked out of existence.

"No!" Horc screamed and fired arrow after arrow as fast as he could at as many Yeti's as he could. He was moving faster than he ever had before in the game. It was like he'd activated some special Ranger power to let him fire that fast. Yetis fell as he struck them multiple times before they could move out of the way. A haze of red enveloped him. There was nothing around him but the Yetis who needed to die. Horc killed them all until there were no more to shoot.

"Horc, Dude, it's okay." Bigdaddybear's hand rested on Horc's shoulder. "You've taken them all out."

"Or scared them off," Titanya said.

Horc shook his head. "I don't think these things controlled by the AI can be scared off. They're in the fight until the end."

"I agree." Tufkakes said appearing on top of one of the boulders. Jamica appeared out of the shadows just below him. "But we, or better yet, Horc, got them all. No more Yetis in the area."

Horc looked at Bigdaddybear. "Check with Rick and see if they managed to get Scarletcrest. Did he get out, or we have to add him to our list of people to rescue?"

Pursing his lips and wrinkling his nose, Bigdaddybear nodded.

"Man, they were more spread out than I thought," Theodore said.

Wolf came over and nudged Horc's hand for a scratch. "And more of them than you said," Horc replied. He'd lost a party member and he wasn't sure who to be mad at. He hadn't thought to have anyone watching their back. Maybe if he had then they'd have spotted the Yetis coming in from behind. But if the Yetis had been anticipating their arrival, it might not have done any good. There were only so many of them, and when an entire tribe of humanoids attacked them, all they could do was their best and hope nobody got killed.

"Sorry about that," Theodore sounded sincere in his sadness. "I hope he got out."

"He did," Bigdaddybear said. "Rick says Scarletcrest is safe out of the game, and free of his pod. He listened to our instructions and logged out as soon as he started to respawn."

That took a lot of the weight of Horc's shoulders. "Thanks. That's good to hear."

"Night's getting close," Baladara said, her health and mana bars already showing full. "Should we find a spot to camp, or do you want to keep going and use magical light to guide us?"

"We don't know how long before these things respawn," Horc said after taking a moment to consider their limited options. "Let's keep going. I hate to say it, but unless we can find a safe spot in the trees, or caves, we might be on the move until we actually defeat the Dragon."

"Then I'm going to worry about all of us getting fatigued," Baladara said. "We're going to need somewhere to rest, but I also agree that here where we just killed a tribe of Yetis isn't the best option for us."

Horc glanced at Theodore and Tufkakes. "Can you two find us somewhere safe to sleep? We'll post a watch, one caster and one tank per watch."

Titanya looked at Stanoran. "I can take first watch on the tank side."

Stanoran nodded as they all started walking on through the pass. "Sounds good."

It was great how well the guild worked together. It made him feel even worse about the loss of Scarletcrest. The fact that he was alive IRL didn't really help the dark mood that settled over Horc. He wished Scarletcrest was still there with them. He'd been willing to take on the risky journey even when he didn't have to. Being torn apart by Yetis couldn't have been a pleasant way to die, especially with the pods transferring the pain from the digital world to the player's real body.

Horc also wished he knew what had happened when he'd… gone berserk? That was the only term he could think of for what happened. He recalled some of Steelmaiden's berserker rages back in the Gnoll King's dungeon. The problem with that was he hadn't activated any spell, and he wasn't a Barbarian. He didn't want any more mysteries in Halfworld. He wanted to follow the arrow to the AI's Dragon avatar, kill it, and get everyone the AI had kidnapped and set them free so Rick and the other developers could go over the AIs code with a fine-toothed comb to figure out what went wrong and stop it from happening again.

11

THINGS STAYED cold beyond the pass and through the thick forest on the other side. Horc was thankful it wasn't a jungle. They weren't having to hack and slash their way through the underbrush, but at times the trees were so thick they had to ride single file, and duck under branches to make it through. None of them seemed to be in a talkative mood as they went. They'd lost Scarletcrest. Even though he'd been able to log out before the AI got hold of him after his death, it didn't help Horc's mood a whole lot. He was the leader of the guild and was supposed to help provide them guidance and safety. Scarletcrest had been the smallest of them, and in some ways, a Witch was a weaker class than the others, being reliant on more spell components with longer casting times than the Mages like Baladara. The exchange for Witches came in the sheer power of the spells they could cast. But that power hadn't been sufficient to save Scarletcrest when his guild… Horc… had failed to keep him safe enough to bring his power to bear against their opponents. He should've been safe at the back of the party, but he wasn't.

The trees ended and a long pebbled beach greeted them. The ocean was different than it had been at the edge of the desert. It was clearer and looked a lot colder just in the color of the waves and the way they sparkled in the sunshine.

"So now what?" Theodore asked as they started riding along the rocky beach.

"Now we see if we can find a boat," Bigdaddybear said. "There should be some kind of boat, raft, barge, something. Rick said he was working on transport to get us across the water to the AI's lair."

Horc glanced at the arrow on the map, it was still pointing due north. He hoped they weren't going to have to search forever for their aquatic transportation. He felt more exposed on the beach than he had in the forest, even though he knew in the forest there were a lot more places for things to hide and jump out at them. Since they'd fought the Yetis things had been quiet. Not even a rabid squirrel had come out after them.

Wolf rubbed against Horc's leg as they walked along. The red lizard had gotten over its initial jumping every time Wolf did that. It was like the digital companion could sense his discomfort at losing Scarletcrest and was determined to stay close and provide comfort. His constant presence made Horc wonder again what it would be like to have a dog IRL. Would it be as loyal and loving as Wolf was? Would it sense his moods and be there for him, even when no one else was?

"Hey is that it?" Jamica pointed down the beach.

Putting a hand over his eyes to shield from the glare coming off the water, Horc followed her gesture. There was something half in and half out of the water a short distance away. It looked a lot like a huge log sticking out of the ocean. He activated one of his Ranger abilities of Sure Sight to give him a longer look at the thing. Upon closer inspection, it looked to be a Viking longboat with a snarling wolf masthead that bore a striking resemblance to Wolf. There was a woman standing next to it. Horc couldn't make out the text over her head, but it was green, not yellow or red. She looked like some kind of Valkyrie.

"Might be. Looks like we have a friendly along with it," he said as they all kicked their mounts to a faster pace toward the boat.

"Friendly?" Baladara asked. "How is that possible? I thought they locked down the game for people logging back in."

"Maybe they let Scarletcrest generate a new toon and get back in when they sent us a boat," Tufkakes suggested.

The thought of Scarletcrest coming back in a new toon, helped lift Horc's spirits. He would apologize for not being there for the Gnome, and hope nothing happened to his new toon.

"You know, a Viking longboat wasn't exactly what I was thinking when Rick said he'd send a boat," Bigdaddybear said. "I really wish we'd been able to make use of that pirate boat we captured on the way to the arena, but after we escaped the island and were back on the mainland, we tried to get it to work, but couldn't even get it to materialize. I'm betting that was because of the AI."

"The thing about having something like the AI in charge of an environment like this game is that it makes the perfect scapegoat for everything that goes wrong," Theodore said. "But things like equipment not working right, not getting loot or XP, those things are definitely things we can blame on the AI."

Tufkakes laughed. "Yeah sometimes it's nice to actually be able to blame God and have it be the real cause and not our own stupidity."

Horc sighed as they got close enough to be able to make out the green text over the woman standing at the boat. **Miranda, Human, Barbarian, Level 50.**

"It's Miranda," he forced out.

Baladara stared at Horc. "The pod tech? That Miranda?"

Horc shrugged. "Not sure, but probably. She's got text over her head this time. That's not something she's had before."

"Yeah, that Miranda," Bigdaddybear said. "Just got a text from Rick. Since it's all in caps, I'm going to presume he's pissed about it, but he said Bordeaux, the head of Pod support, is with our boat."

Horc's heart sank. He wasn't in the mood to have one of the techs, particularly Miranda, in the game helping them. She wasn't his favorite person in the world, and he was fairly sure she was just going to screw things up.

Miranda waved to them as they rode closer. "Hey guys, I brought you a boat."

Horc reined in his lizard, kicking up a few pebbles as it came to a stop. "Thanks. Why the difference in your appearance this time?" He cut right to the chase. From dealing with her before, he wasn't in the mood to beat around the bush.

She gestured down her body. "Like it? The AI has found a way to block the techs from getting in as techs, and basically having the same power level as it has, so my only option was to come in as a player. After losing your Gnome, I figured you could use another hand."

Titanya walked up to Miranda and put her hands on her hips. "Do you know how to use that toon to the best of its ability? She looks rather flashy to me."

"A bit." Miranda shrugged. "I made a few mods to the toon to help me stay alive. Extra magic items and that such. Oh, I also brought some more healing potions. They've been modified too. No cool downs, so you can use as many as you have to so you can stay alive." She lifted a bag from the long boat.

"That's helpful," Baladara took the bag and pulled out potions and started shoving them in her bag.

"Anything to help with the real world mental damage this game is causing?"

Miranda screwed up her face. "What do you mean?" She stared at Baladara. "Wait, you're using gloves and goggles, you shouldn't be at risk of any real world consequences."

Baladara huffed. "Tell that to Mike. When the spell feedback hit him, it left him a mess. I had to put him to bed and take over to help keep Horc safe." She handed the bag to Tufkakes. "This AI is getting more dangerous. Sister, this isn't just a game anymore, and you better hope you can contribute to this team's success and not be a hindrance. Horc's already hurting from losing one party member, I don't want to see him hurting 'cause he tried and failed to keep your incompetence safe."

Horc thought about getting between them for a split second, then decided to let Baladara have her say. She obviously had things she wanted to get off her chest, and Miranda was a good target for her.

Miranda let out a long breath. "There's apparently a lot we're still learning about this AI. It's a good thing we haven't opened the game to the public yet."

Baladara's face flashed red. "Still learning?" She lunged toward Miranda.

Tufkakes thrust the bag of potions to Jamica and grabbed Baladara. "Girl, it ain't worth it. We can use the extra muscle right now. Wait till we get out of here and hit her IRL…it'll be more satisfying."

"Okay." Baladara relaxed and turned away from Miranda. "Thanks TK. But I don't think she could bring assault charges for something that happens in game."

"Maybe not, but right now we need her and her boat." Tufkakes took Baladara by the arm and led her toward the back of the boat.

Horc looked at Miranda who looked more than a little confused by Baladar's outburst. "Okay. Now that

that's over, do you know how to drive this thing, and where we're going?"

Miranda pointed over the edge of the boat. There were rows of seats, each with a small clockwork Viking in it. "These guys power it. According to Remington, they're steam powered and magical, so they shouldn't be able to be taken over by the AI like NPC rowers would."

Horc peered closer at them, and each one was like a toy Viking, complete with horned helmet, beards, and axes. They reminded him of toys he'd seen in a store during some movie release, but they were shinier.

"Oh, my," Stanoran said. "They're so cute. Too bad we can't each take one home after this is done. They'd be great replacements for Elf on a Shelf."

Rambull frowned. "You really don't get out much, do you Stanoran? Elf on a Shelf is so ten years ago."

Horc sighed, ready for things to get wrapped up. "Okay, then, I guess we need to get someone to push us into the ocean, turn these little guys on, and get moving."

Baladara climbed over the side of the boat. "That's tank work." She walked to a row of seats in the back and sat down with her arms crossed. She might've relaxed on some level, but it was obvious she was still pissed at Miranda.

"Stanoran and I can get that," Titanya said.

"Or Stanoran and I can get it," Rambull countered.

Titanya frowned at the big Minotauren. "Let's not get sexist here."

Rambull spread his hands and shook his head. "Not sexist, just Stanoran and I are the largest."

Stanoran hopped over the edge of the boat and went to sit near Baladara. "You realize we've got two Ursans who are fairly large too."

Horc shook his head. "Titanya, do you mind helping me push the boat out. Everyone else get in." He glanced at Wolf. "You too. I'll be there in a second."

Titanya grinned as she walked to the front of the boat. "Let's do this."

Once everyone was in the longboat, Horc put his hands on the side of it near the masthead and started pushing. The pebbles covering the beach shifted under his feet, and he slipped the first couple of steps. Then he found his footing, and with Titanya on the other side of the masthead, pushed the boat out into the water until it was floating easily.

"Here." Bigdaddybear reached down for Horc's hand.

Horc took it and Bigdaddybear easily lifted him into the boat. On the other side, Theodore was hauling Titanya in.

A bit of movement on shore drew Horc's attention to the lizard mounts there. He wondered if they should've unsaddled them instead of just letting them go. He figured if the AI wasn't acting up, the mounts would've magically gone into their bags or something so they could be reused again. In his rational brain, he knew they were just digital creations of the game, but the red lizard had felt so alive during all his interactions with it, even when it had freaked out when the Dragons attacked.

"The game will reabsorb them soon," Bigdaddybear said, as if he was understanding Horc's long look at the shore. "It would be nice to keep them. It was better than walking everywhere, and the lizards fit this body better than a horse would've."

Rambull laughed. "Exactly. I can't see me or either of you Ursans on horses. That would look ridiculous, and probably be awkward as well. Since Halfworld is more complex than other games, we have to think about things like size ratios and all."

"Not something I would've thought of," Miranda said, walking up the aisle of mini metal Vikings who were moving the oars along to propel them across the ocean.

"Your specialty is the pods we game in," Horc said. "The actual game dynamics are handled by other departments. One of the things that make these games work so well is everyone working together to make things happen. Without a team, none of this would be possible."

He paused. Would he have been able to even contemplate taking on the AI without the team that had formed around him? A few days earlier, he was fighting to stay alive in the game, but after his life was no longer at stake, other people's were. Somehow that made things so much more of a reality for him.

"I hope we don't have to deal with pirates again," Bigdaddybear said. "I don't think a longboat would be good for fighting off pirates."

"Pirates." Tufkakes frowned, making her mask-like markings droop and look like running paint. "Yeah, I don't want to deal with those guys again."

Horc nodded. "It would be nice if things went smoothly, at least for a little while."

"Second that." Jamica leaned against the railing of the boat, then she glanced at Miranda. "I guess you didn't think to bring heavy cloaks for everyone."

Miranda glanced at her own heavy furs, then frowned. "I can't really think of everything."

"I guess you can't." Horc turned and looked back where Baladara, Stanoran, Theodore and Rambull sat on the bench behind the mini rowers. Baladara still looked pissed, and he wondered how long, Lisa would hold a grudge against Miranda. He just hoped it wasn't going to cause a problem on their quest. He needed his team working together. Then he realized Miranda wasn't part of the guild or party. He quickly sent her a guild invite and added her to the party. They were going to need that to give them all an extra edge by having her as part of the guild.

Baladara's frown deepened and Horc knew she'd seen Miranda appear on her screen as part of the party. Yeah, this was going to be a lot of fun.

12

THE ARROW on Horc's map still pointed north, but the edge of the island they approached was a sheer cliff rising several hundred feet. The waves slashed against the rocks, sending spray up.

Titanya stood next to Horc in the front of the ship, looking at the cliff. "Well, this doesn't look good."

Horc shook his head, then ran his hand through his hair. "You're right. I guess it was too much to hope that we could just land the boat on a nice beach, get off and then go storm the AI's lair."

"Yeah, I think you're asking for a lot with that." Titanya grinned. "Let's check the game map and see if it will tell us where to put ashore."

"Probably won't do us much good," Bigdaddybear said from next to them. "None of us have been here yet. The map hasn't filled in for any of us."

Miranda cleared her throat. "In an attempt to be helpful, I had one of Punjabi's people make sure I had full access to the maps. Mine's as complete as it can be." She closed her eyes for a moment.

Horc had noticed that Miranda closed her eyes when accessing things in her game menu, like having the overlay of the menu with her vision of what was going on in the game was hard for her to process. It was a sign she wasn't as hardcore a gamer as a lot of people he knew. He was thankful he hadn't had to do that when he started. It was such a newb move.

After a couple of seconds, Miranda blinked. "Okay. If I read things right, we need to go left…ah west…along the shore. There's a beach about a quarter of the way around the continent where we can land. If we go right, the first accessible landing is a bit farther away."

Horc frowned. "Continent? I thought this was an island."

Miranda shrugged and walked up to the little metal Viking that seemed to control the boat. "It's not a large continent; I guess you could call it a huge island. What do you consider Ausrtaila? An island or a continent?"

With a huff, Horc sagged his shoulders. The time to get to the AI dragon's lair was growing longer, not shorter. The more time it took to get there, the more the AI was going to know and the harder it was going to be to defeat.

"Anything else we should know?" Bigdaddybear asked as the rowers turned the boat and headed along the cliffs to the west. The sun was low, basically sitting on the water ahead of them.

"Know?" Miranda shrugged. "Not sure what else there is to know. That's the closest place for us to put in."

Horc walked over to the bench in the front of the boat, sat there and crossed his arms. He hoped he might get a little sleep while night fell and they made their way to the landing spot. Wolf curled up under his feet, again providing a level of comfort to him as the boat moved easily through the waves.

"IT'S BEEN following us for a while," Tufkakes said, pointing to a wake moving between the ship and the cliffs. In the early morning light, it was fairly obvious.

Horc frowned. "No sign as to what it is?" He couldn't see anything besides the water disturbed by the passage of something underneath it.

Tufkakes shook his head. "It was there when I got up to stretch at first light. I've been watching it, and so far it hasn't done anything but parallel our course."

"If we were on land, I'd go check it out," Bigdaddybear said leaning against the rail next to Horc. "But out in the ocean, I've got no spells or anything to help out. Ursans might be more attuned to water than Sand Elves, but I think we'd need a Selkie or some kind of aquatic troll to really be much good here."

"We can play Selkies?" Horc kept realizing there was a lot about Halfworld he didn't know, and wished he'd done more than just randomly roll up his toon. But even with that thought, he didn't want to make major changes to himself. He liked being a Half Orc Ranger. He reached down and rubbed Wolf's head where his companion sat at his feet.

"Yeah." Tufkakes nodded. "I think I heard rumors of lots more races before the game goes live to the public."

"They're drawing things from all sort of fantasy worlds, legends, and more," Bigdaddybear said. "I think they've got lots planned for the next few expansions too. They want to do a lot more to keep players interested. The more people play, the more money the company makes."

A long reptilian neck rose out of the water followed by a huge hump.

"Why does it look like the Loch Ness Monster?" Titanya asked. "Everyone knows Nessie doesn't exist."

"We don't know that for sure," Tufkakes countered.

"IRL doesn't count." Horc's heart pounded as the sea serpent turned and headed toward the longboat. "Miranda, how close are we to the beach?" He wanted options, and fighting a huge sea monster from a small Viking longboat didn't sound like a very good option.

"Not far. We could swim if we had to," Miranda replied.

"We don't want to do that," Horc said. If there was one thing he really didn't want to do was swim in waters infested with sea monsters.

"We might want to start defending the ship then," Baladara said as she began casting her spell, making her hands glow bright red.

Horc targeted the monster. Its text was red. **Seamonsaur Level 50**.

The first arrow to hit it was a Fire impact arrow. The damage it did appeared negligible. The others' attacks followed close on his, then the Seamonsaur broadsided their boat.

Horc managed to hold onto his bow, and only the magic of his quiver kept him from losing arrows as he tumbled backward, hitting his back on the boat's deck and nearly being thrown overboard on the far railing; that wasn't as far as it sounded. His health bar flashed as a little bit of damage registered from his fall.

"Hang on!" Titanya shouted as she raised her massive sword and leaped at the Seamonsaur. Her second blow did almost no damage to the aquatic beast, but she kept swinging. Baladara's magical attacks didn't seem like they had much impact either, but like the sandstorm, they were working at whittling it down, bit by bit.

"Help!" Stanoran voice came from somewhere behind Horc.

Horc glanced around. The Priest had fallen overboard and was frantically paddling to keep his head above water. The water beyond the boat was fairly calm, but near the boat, the actions of the Seamonsaur were making for rough seas.

Glancing around, Horc spotted several ropes curled around long wooden pins at the edge of the deck. He shouldered his bow as he ran to the nearest rope. The sea serpent hit the boat again, sending Horc sliding into the railing. He grabbed hold and managed not to join

Stanoran in the surf. The rope was wet from the ocean spray. Horc fumbled as the Seamonsaur roared and again thrashed against the boat.

Glancing over the railing, there no sign of the Priest in the waves. "Stanoran!" Horc frantically uncoiled the rope.

Tufkakes appeared at his side. "I'm not much help against that thing."

"Stanoran went overboard." Horc wrapped the end of the rope around his waist. "I'm going after him."

"Let me." Tufkakes put his hand on Horc's. "I bet Procyans are better swimmers than Half Orcs."

Horc didn't like the idea of someone else putting themselves in the line of danger he could handle, but it made sense. He had no idea how well he could swim. Horc unwound the end of the rope and handed it to Tufkakes. "Be careful."

"Always." Tufkakes dove off the railing and into the water as Horc tied the other end of the rope to the heavy pin it had been wrapped around.

Horc wanted to keep an eye on things and make sure both Tufkakes and Stanoran got out of the water okay, but the others might need his help too. He pulled his bow back out and focused on the Seamonsaur. It was only down a little under three quarters of its health.

With a tight focus, Horc managed to get a Fire arrow into the thing's eye. Titanya hung onto her massive sword that was embedded into the monster's shoulder as she fought to get it out. Baladara sent several Fireballs as Horc fired more arrows. Wolf was dangling from under the sea serpent's jaw, where he'd latched on and was raking his claws into its throat, leaving deepening bloody scratches with each second. Miranda had some kind of beam shooting out of a javelin.

The rope next to Horc jerked tight. Horc turned to stare at where the hemp strand disappeared into the water. There was no sign of either Tufkakes or Stanoran. He jerked on the rope.

Pull us up. Tufkakes. Appeared in group text.

Again shouldering his bow, Horc bent to the task, pulling hand over hand, hauling his teammates up through the monster-roughed sea. He wasn't going to lose either one of them like he'd lost Scarletcrest.

His muscles burned after a couple of minutes, and he wished one of the others was there to help, but they were all busy trying to bring down the beast attacking their boat.

He glanced at the team icons. Stanoran's health was flashing red, then went back to green as his mana dropped a bit. Tufkakes was down over half way, but still had enough to survive the trip to the surface.

The boat shook violently, and wood splintered.

Horc scrambled to keep his footing as the wet rope slipped through his fingers, burning as it went. He caught himself on the rail again. It slammed hard into his stomach leaving him gasping hard as he pitched toward the water. The rope snapped tight against the pin, pinching Horc's arm between it and the rail. "Damn it." His health dropped again.

It took all his strength to free his arm and get the rope moving again. As he worked, he watched his team's icons. Titanya's health started flashing orange, then shot back up into the green. Rambull's mana was down, but his health was strong, Baladara was in the same state. Tufkakes' health dropped into the red, then returned to full. Stanoran's mana was under half. He was obviously casting healing on both himself and Tufkakes to give Horc a chance to get them to the surface.

Horc worked hand over hand, hoping the team was taking down the monster faster than it was taking them down. He wanted to get everyone on deck so he could make sure they were safe, and so he could lend his arrows to the fight. His own health started dropping faster as his muscles screamed at the effort to get Tufkakes and Stanoran out of the water. Even as his stomach complained about the abuse, he leaned on the rail to give him something solid to pull against. The deck was so wet from the constant pitching and splashing it was nearly impossible for him to balance properly and be able to pull.

The Seamonsaur roared again and thrashed against the boat. Horc scrambled to keep his feet as his side of the boat dipped toward the ocean, then it suddenly rocked the other way, tossing him into the sky. His shoulder screamed in agony as he reached the end of the rope and the weight of his teammates, and the ocean jerked him to a stop. He was down to nealy half health.

Something snapped at him. Horc dangled from the rope, just inches from the Seamonsaur's jaws. Wolf was there, with his teeth still buried in the monster's flesh and kicking and clawing for all he was worth. Horc spun on the rope, dangling from the railing, and managed to swing out and behind the Seamonsaur's neck. Below him Titanya and Theodore were hacking away at it. Horc got the rope around the monster's neck and let momentum carry him around for another time. He was just below where Wolf was working on savaging the thing.

When the boat splashed back down into the water, the Seamonsaur did the work of pulling Tufkakes and Stanoran back into the air. Stanoran dropped to the deck, landing in a heap and not moving as Tufkakes dangled from the rope that was still tied around his waist.

Horc pulled out his dagger and sliced into the monster's neck, sliding down toward its back as he let go of the rope. When he landed on the thing's shoulder, just a few feet from Titanya, his health dropped to under a quarter from the impact. The monster was down into the orange, but Horc worried they might not have enough in them left to finish it.

Tufkakes kicked off the thing's neck and swung around, even as it bent to try to catch him in its jaws. Pulling out his own dagger, Tufkakes arched up and caught the thing in the back of the head. The blow must've been at such an angle to give the Rogue a Backstab bonus as it knocked the monster into the red. Then concentrated attacks from the casters finished it off.

One second, Horc was standing on the thing's back, the next, the Seamonsaur pixelated, vanished and he was dropping into the water. Wolf and Titanya were right there with him as Theodore and Rambull immediately started swimming toward the side of the boat.

Ignoring the protest of his arms, Horc grabbed hold of Titanya and hauled her toward the boat. In her chainmail, she was as apt to sink as swim. He'd already seen what platemail would do in the ocean and had no doubts that chainmail could be just as bad.

There was a splash next to him, and Tufkakes surfaced, dragging the rope behind him. "Okay. I don't want to do that ever again."

"Yeah." Was all Horc could force out between gasps for air. His own health was dropping quickly from the abuse he was dealing out to his body. He wanted to get back to the boat and sit and rest for a little while.

"Here!" Bigdaddybear lean over the rail and reached a huge paw-like hand down.

Rambull reached him first send was pulled out, then Theodore. Horc helped Titanya out as Tufkakes scrambled up the side of the boat without help. Then he paused and looked at Wolf paddling desperately next to him.

"This isn't going to be the most dignified thing." Horc lifted the wolf up. His arms felt like lead and complained at the action. It was all he could do to heft

Wolf far enough that Bigdaddybear could grab him by the scruff and get him out.

Horc's health was flashing red. His leg and arms were trying their best to not respond to what he needed them to do. He was so tired he wanted nothing more than to stop struggling and sink into the waves, but if he did that, then who would stop the AI and rescue the hostages?

Two huge hairy paw-hands grabbed him.

"We got him!" Theodore shouted.

Then they hauled Horc onto the deck, and he collapsed. His health was flashing red and he closed his eyes, hoping one of the healers noticed his situation.

13

HORC CAME to with a start. He was wet, soaked to the skin, and lying on a sopping deck. Something nearby was hissing horribly, and the deck was lurching like mad.

"What happened?" He sat up and rubbed his eyes.

Bigdaddybear stared down at him. "You nearly died is what happened. I don't think it was programmed into the game originally, but apparently one of the upgrades the AI has given us is that if we push our physical bodies too hard, we start taking damage. Combined with the hits the sea monster gave you, we almost didn't get you healed in time. You can thank Stanoran for the healing. I was too busy hauling your soggy butt out of the water."

"Can we not worry about that right now, we're about to sink," Miranda complained.

Horc shot to his feet. "About to sink?" His head spun slightly from the sudden movement. He squared his shoulders and did his best to not show weakness to the others.

Miranda rolled her eyes. "Yeah, you didn't think we could take all the fighting with that thing and not sustain damage to the boat, did you?"

"What can we do?" Horc ran through everyone's skills. Their magics were battle or healing based, since that was how the game was set up. "Bigdaddybear, do you have any Druid spells that could help? Entangling roots that might bind the boat together for a little while? How about our shamans, anything there?"

Bigdaddybear got a thoughtful look on his face. "You know, that might actually work. It's an area of effect spell at this level, so I don't need a target per'se. Let's see if I can hit the deck of the boat with it and then get the vines to wrap around the railings to pull things together."

"See what happens." Horc glanced at Theodore and Rambull.

The two of them shook their heads.

"We're more spiritual," Theodore explained, then a thoughtful look crossed his face. "Wait a minute. I've got a Summon Water Spirit spell. Maybe I can get it to keep the boat afloat as we try to get to land."

Rambull sighed. "I took Summon Earth Spirit, I don't think that will…" his voice trailed off. "I might be able to provide us with a stable spot for a few minutes."

Horc pointed at Theodore. "Do your spell; get the water spirit to hold us up while Bigdaddybear tries to hold us together."

At that point, thorny vines erupted on the deck of the boat and spread out from their center point. Bigdaddybear's face was set in concentration, and the patch of vines slowly narrowed and reached for the railings, then over them. The boat creaked, then shifted slightly.

Theodore's hands glowed light blue, then watery fingers appeared on either side of the boat. "Okay, we got this, but only for a few minutes."

"Can we get the rowers moving?" Horc asked, then realized that the whistling and puffing he'd been hearing was coming from the mini Vikings. Several of them were belching steam and missing strokes as they went through their clockwork motions.

"They're trying," Miranda retorted. "They took some damage too."

"Beach ho!" Baladara shouted from the front of the boat.

Horc let out a long huff. "Hang together a few more minutes." He stood in the middle of the boat and watched the shore come closer and closer as the cliff fell away.

A small village was a short distance down the shore.

"We need to tuck in as tight to the cliff as possible." Horc said. "If we can avoid conflict with the village, that would be awesome." He'd been through enough fighting for a few hours, even if the fight with the Seamonsaur hadn't lasted too long, and hoped they could avoid more. Since a village normally meant NPCs, and the last few NPCs they'd encountered hadn't been friendly, he wanted to give them as wide a berth as possible.

"Steering's not great," Miranda said. "Between the damage and the water spirit pushing us along."

"I'll get us in," Theodore said. He glanced toward the shore and frowned. "Yeah this might be tight. Everyone better be ready to run."

Horc nodded. "Alright, everyone to the front of the boat. Get ready to disembark."

The shore approached quickly, and Horc was sure they were going to hit harder and faster than was probably safe. This beach looked like gray sand instead of the pebbles that had been on the beach they'd launched from. The water spirit let go of the boat and the craft slowly eased up on its velocity as it approached shore, but more water was rising up through the lower parts of the boat. It looked like things were going to be close.

"Can't hold it any longer," Bigdaddybear said as the boat hit a sandbar and began disintegrating.

"Everyone make a run for it." Horc suddenly found himself knee-deep in ocean water. Around him the rest of the party ran for the shore. He followed close behind with Wolf at his side.

As Horc staggered onto shore, once again more tired than he wanted to admit, the sounds of drums rolled across the beach.

"We need to keep running," Horc urged. It was enough that they had attracted the attention of the locals, he hoped they could outdistance them, and barring that, at least have the NPCs be a sufficiently low level to be easily defeated.

"Right behind you, boss," Tufkakes replied. "Although I'd really like to have time to get my fur dry."

"Lots of luck with that right now," Baladara sniped as the two splashed onto shore. "This whole day is one big soaking mess."

Horc kept his mouth shut as the rest of the party made it to dry land. "Head up the hillside as fast as possible. Bigdaddybear, you're in lead, I'll bring up the rear." He knew there was danger behind them, he just hoped Bigdaddybear would be keen enough to catch any trouble they might stumble across in their mad rush to avoid the villagers as the drums became louder and more demanding.

Several NPC's emerged from crude gray dwellings. He was fairly sure the red text above their heads said Ice Trolls. As much as he wracked his brain, Horc couldn't recall is Ice Trolls were fast or slow, or how persistent they would be while chasing them. With the AI in control of NPCs, it was nearly impossible to tell how long the villagers would chase them.

14

HORC FROWNED as they stopped on at the base of a hill in the rolling tundra that lay between them and the AI dragon. Tufkakes rubbed his hands together and blew on them before he continued recounting the scouting run he and Jamiaca had just returned from.

"We can't find any way to get around them, without going back the way we came," Tufkakes explained. "I'm willing to bet the AI moved these NPCs into the valley specifically to block our way."

"But we can't go back without hitting those Ice Trolls who've been following us since we left the beach," Horc said. He was already nervous about pausing long enough to make a plan. That was probably how the AI had everything worked out. Keep pressure on them from behind, and get them caught between two groups of powerful opponents.

"None of this looks very good." Bigdaddybear squatted down in the rough brown lichens that covered the rocky ground.

"What about going over those hills over there?" Baladara pointed to the southeast. "I know it'll take us out of our way, but isn't that better than getting caught in a scissor movement?"

"I think you mean pincer maneuver," Stanoran muttered.

Baladara glared at him. "Whatever."

Horc nodded. "You've got a point there. Unfortunately, we don't know what lies that way. It might be another group of NPCs and then where would we be?"

"Same place we are now," Bigdaddybear said. "If the group in the valley is just waiting for us to come through there, then we aren't going to have to worry about them coming after us like the ones from the beach are." He nodded thoughtfully. "Let's go that way. Worst thing that happens is we find a larger force than the one they spotted in the valley."

Tufkakes took a long breath, blowing hard on his hands, then looked at Jamica. "You ready to run again? Man it would've been nice if we still had the lizards."

"Sorry Rick couldn't find a way to make them part of our gear like regular mounts." Bigdaddybear shrugged. "Maybe after they get the AI reset."

"So many maybes." Jamica said as she turned in the direction they'd all be going. "Good thing we're both excellent runners. Come on fuz, see who can get to the top of the next hill first." And the Troll Rogue took off running as a fast jog.

"We'll be back." Tufkakes grinned and followed her.

Horc cast one last look in the direction his quest wanted him to go, then started off after the two rogues. He still felt odd letting the Rogues do the scouting. That was a Ranger's job. But as guild leader, he also needed to be the one making decisions, and protecting his people. That meant staying with the main force in case the Ice Trolls caught up to them. They'd been lucky, and the NPCs weren't as fast as players. He hoped that would stay the case.

THEY MADE it to the top of the next hill, leaving a swatch of smashed lichen across the tundra. Tufkakes dashed up from the other side, huffing.

He paused and put his hands on his knees, trying to catch his breath. "We've got critters all over the place. Mostly bears."

"Bears?" Horc asked.

"Yeah, massed at the base of the next hill over." Tufkakes took a long breath, as if to still his breathing. "I've never seen that many critters gathered together in a game before. Has to be twenty or thirty of them, just standing there like robots who are waiting for the power to be turned on. Kinda creepy. I'm also getting tired of physical exertion impacting health. I lost a quarter getting back to you guys."

"Here." Stanoran's hands glowed blue, and in the party icons, Tufkakes' health bar filled.

"Thanks." Tufkakes gave him a quick grin.

"Seems like no matter which way we go, we're going to encounter resistance," Titanya said. "Which do we think will be easier, critters or NPCs?"

"Critters," several of them said at once.

Horc wasn't sure how he felt about beating up on a bunch of animals to get across the landscape, but then he reminded himself they were just bits in a computer program. They'd come back as they were originally meant to be. It wasn't a huge deal.

"Okay. Let's take out the bears and friends." Horc looked up to the hill. "I might even have an idea. It's something I haven't tried before, but I see it here on my spell list."

Baladara looked at him and rubbed the pommel of her short sword. "What are you thinking?"

"Traps," Horc explained as he started walking toward the next hill. "I've got a couple of different trap spells I can set. Maybe if I put them in a line, we can have a couple of people go down and get the bears to charge up the hill and get caught in the traps." He selected a Blazing Pit Trap and looked at its information.

"Says in the trap description that they immobilize anything caught in them for five seconds."

"That's not much time," Rambull said from behind Horc. "But if the rest of us are ready with our attacks, it might help take an initial amount of damage off them. Does the spell impact just one mob, or is it an AOE?"

"Area of Effect," Horc said, then checked the two other trap spells he had but hadn't used. They were similar, but with different results. One was ice, and the other was concussion. The Concussion Trap had a longer time than the ensnared were immobilized, ten seconds.

"Can you cast multiple traps at one time?" Theodore asked.

"I think," Horc read back through the spell descriptions and it wasn't clear if they could be active at the same time or not. They all only lasted up to five minutes, more than enough time to lure some bears into them. "Won't know until we try."

"Exactly." Baladara said. "I've also got a couple of delayed spells we can try. So far we haven't had opportunity to try any."

"Barbarians also have trap spells," Miranda said.

"Let's try this and see what happens," Bigdaddybear agreed. "So why don't Theodore, Rambull and I go down and draw some agro and then get to the top of the hill with bears in hot pursuit? Gee, it'll be like a night at the bar."

"You go to different bars than I do," Baladara said.

"No doubt." Bigdaddybear laughed.

As they reached the backside of the hill, Bigdaddybear, Theodore, and Rambull headed around the base of it, while Horc, and the others headed toward the top to set the traps.

"I've got a couple of trap spells too," Tufkakes said as they hurried up to the top. "Let me check with Jamica and see if she took the right talent tree to get them too."

Nothing appeared in party chat as Tufkakes messaged their guild member who hadn't come back with him when he returned from the scouting mission. Horc assumed she was somewhere nearby waiting for something to happen.

Tufkakes shook his head. "She's on the Assassin Tree. But she said she'd help the others draw the bears up to us."

"Good." Horc paused as they approached the top of the hill. "So what do you all think? Along the top, or just down from it? If just down, which side of the hill?"

A thoughtful line appeared on Baladara's forehead. "Just down from the top, and on the other side."

"Sounds decent to me," Miranda said.

"To give us high ground," Titanya agreed with a stiff nod.

"As long as the others don't agro them too fast." Horc hurried over the top of the hill, and started down the other side before he came to a stop and stared. Tufkakes had said twenty to thirty bears. What he saw at the base of the hill had to be more than that.

"Let's not stop and stare," Baladara said. "We need to move fast."

Horc shook himself out of staring at assembled mob below them. He huffed once, and set about to casting the trap spells. Baladara and Tufkakes did the same.

As he selected the Fire Pit Trap spell, Horc's hands glowed red and seemed to move of their own accord. The ground in front of him rolled slightly, and a soft red haze covered it. When he stepped back, it looked a bit like the fields of lava that had been all over the news when the volcanoes wiped out Hawaii a few years earlier. If the bears spotted the odd ground, he wondered if they'd avoid it, or just charge through it.

The Ice Trap spell had a similar effect, although it was more like a layer of frost spreading across the tundra.

Other than a slight shimmer that looked a lot like a heat wave, there wasn't anything showing on the surface of the ground after he finished casting the Concussion Trap spell.

"Here they come!" Titanya shouted.

Horc stopped staring at the ground and looked up as Theodore, Bigdaddybear and Rambull charged toward them with most of the bears in hot pursuit.

"Get over there," Baladara pointed to the point where her first trap was laid. "Miranda, give them a mark they can use to tell where the traps are."

"I'll mark this side." Tufkakes stood straight where he had placed his last spell.

Horc's traps were in between the others. He stepped back, and realized his mana was showing low. Yanking open his bag, Horc fished out a vial of mana potion.

The hill shook with the thundering pads of a huge mass of things heading his way. Without looking down the slope, Horc opened the vial and knocked it back as Wolf started howling at his side.

He readied an impact arrow, adding a bit of Fire to it and focused his shot in the middle of the Ice Trap.

Bigdaddybear leapt over the Ice Trap and came to a rolling stop just inches from Horc. A huge wave of white and brown bears surged along in his wake. Horc didn't waste any time, he let his arrow fly. It hit the lead bear and exploded in flames just as the critter crossed the border of the Ice Trap.

Swirling ice and snow shot up from the ground, spreading out ten feet or more as it engulfed the bears and wolverines that ran into it. The smaller critters vanished on impact, their health overwhelmed. The bears stopped, frozen and continuing to take damage from the intense cold as they struggled to free themselves.

The Concussion Trap exploded, sending out invisible waves of force at the animals as they ran over it.

Again, the smaller mobs were destroyed instantly, but the larger ones stopped in their tracks, stunned by the force of the blast.

Next to Horc, Bigdaddybear and Baladara got off spells, the bright colored lights of them zipping across the space between the party and the mobs. Their effects weren't as spectacular as the trap spells were, but were still interesting.

Then the Fire Pit Trap erupted. It was like a fountain of flames hit the bears, knocking some back, throwing others forward, and catching all of them on fire. The trap looked like a bunch of fireworks all going off at once, shooting sparks and flames high into the air and immobilizing everything it struck.

Horc fired arrows as fast as he could, adding spells when they were available, and when they weren't just shooting arrow after arrow. Bears fell but there always seemed to be more. He didn't have time to keep track of what his party was doing as he kept his eyes on the opponents coming up the hill. As soon as he and Wolf dropped one, he was looking for his next target. As far as number of targets was concerned, it was the most intense fight he'd been in.

They seemed to keep coming for several minutes, then the flow died down. Horc was out of mana as three bears ran at him. He couldn't add anything to his special arrows, so he picked them carefully. He hit the closest bear with an impact arrow to the eye, then followed that up with a razor arrow. Wolf took out a wolverine, then slammed into the second bear.

Horc backed up, hoping to keep some distance between him and his opponents as his mana regained something, or maybe he could get a mana potion down to add some zip to his arrows. Nearby Rambull bellowed as the ground shook and several bears went flying due to his Charge attack. Then his health bar began to fall rapidly.

Horc glanced over his shoulder toward the last place he'd seen the Shaman, but the only thing that was obvious was a mass of bears mauling something.

"Back off!" Horc had just enough mana for a Multi Shot buff on his arrows. He selected impact arrows and hoped it would buy him the time he needed to get a mana potion down and keep doing more damage.

His arrows hit their marks, and three of the bears turned toward him. Horc's heart pounded as Rambull's health bar flashed red and vanished.

Wolf howled as if he was aware of the fall of their partymate. Horc shot the closest bear, wishing he could do critical hits as the arrow found its mark in the bear's eye. The damage was enough to finish it off, but there were still two more close to him and more behind them.

Lightning danced from the sky, striking several of the bears, staggering one of the ones close to Horc. He hit it with a razor arrow, reducing it to pixels.

Wolf hit the other close one, rolling it down the hill, snarling and snapping as they went. Horc held his breath, but Wolf's health didn't drop very far, and he came out on top of the bear at the end of their roll.

Horc reached back into his pack, feeling for the vials with mana potion. The slightly raised lips on the health potions weren't what he was looking for. Then his fingers found the smooth transition from vial to cork that the mana potions had. He snatched one. With his thumb, he popped the small cork out and it fell to the ground as a bear hit him.

The vial went flying as Horc hit the ground hard. He punched the bear in the snout as hard as he could. Bones broke in both his hand and the bear's nose. The bear roared and staggered backward.

Horc's health was down by nearly a quarter. He yanked out his dagger and went after the bear. He knew he should run back and get to the distance his arrows would work, but it didn't matter. They'd lost another guild member and he wanted the bears to die before they lost another one. If they kept losing members, they wouldn't be able to take on the AI with even a slim chance of winning.

He jabbed at the bear, hitting it again in the wounded nose. His knife sank nearly to the hilt before the bear jerked up with a bellow of pain. Horc held on and yanked the knife down through the roof of the bear's mouth.

Its health bar flashed orange.

The bear swiped its claws into Horc's leg. The force and pain made him stumble backwards and he screamed, more in fury than agony. He threw himself onto the bear's back, and rammed his dagger as deep into its chest as he could.

In a flash of red, the bear's health bar vanished, taking the bear with it.

Horc sprawled on the ground, hoping his wounded leg would support his weight as the sounds of battle died around him before another bear or wolverine got close enough to take him on.

"Dude, lie still." Stanoran touched Horc's shoulder. "You're about to die."

"What?" Horc muttered, then looked at his own health bar. It was strobing red, like it was getting ready to go out. Then Stanoran's healing spell hit him. Warmth spread through his limbs and the pain vanished from his leg. His health bar stopped flashing red and returned to a healthy green as the magic healed him and brought him back to full health.

Horc lay there for a minute as Stanoran went on to someone else. He'd managed to survive as someone in his party died. He wondered what would happen to the hostages if they didn't succeed. Would Total Immersion Systems send another team in, or would it just write off those people held by the AI as collateral damage and pull the plug? He didn't think that would happen, as the company was desperate to avoid bad press, and a bunch of employees dying in their pods was almost guaranteed to provide bad press.

Horc glanced at the party avatars. Everyone was there, except Rambull. He desperately didn't want to be in charge any longer, but their group had come together because of him. They all deferred to him. He wasn't about to let them down, although he felt like he'd let Rambull and Scarletcrest down by not finding a way to keep them alive.

As Stanoran and Bigdaddybear's mana dropped, everyone's health returned to normal. Horc pulled out a chunk of meat and tossed it to Wolf, then did a Companion Heal on him. Things were just going to get tougher as they went along, so they were simply going to have to bear down and keep fighting.

"The Ice Trolls are starting up the hill!" Jamica shouted, jerking Horc's attention behind them.

He'd totally forgotten about the NPCs who'd pursued them across the continent. He had to do better or none of them were going to survive.

15

"HIT THEM hard and fast!" Horc shouted. "We've got the advantage of high ground." He'd never tried to throw traps. The last set of trap spells had been the first ones he'd ever cast. He pulled up the energy for a Fire Pit Trap Spell, then threw it out to make the glow of the spell land in the middle of the Ice Trolls.

The spell sailed through the air like one of Baladara's Fireballs. It hit the ground and instantly spread out along the ground. The effects happened almost before the spell landed. Since it was in the middle of the NPCs charging up the hill at them, it exploded outward catching a group of NPCs up in the blast.

They didn't scream, or roar like the beasts did. They just dissolved into pixels.

Miranda threw her trap spells down the hill. Each one flew down the slope, knocking out Ice Trolls when they landed. Baladara's Fireballs and Magical Force Bolts blazed down on the NPCs. The damage they inflicted barely slowed down the Trolls, having little more effect than Horc's arrows.

"There's too many of them," Bigdaddybear unleashed a ferocious wind at their attackers.

"We can do this!" Miranda pointed her club and unleashed a spout of fire toward the Trolls.

"You're not a gamer, Miranda, you don't get it. There's too many of them." Titanya impaled the first Troll to get through the traps and distance attacks. "We're already worn down from the running and the bears. We can't hold this hill."

"And they're trying to get around to the other side of the hill," Theodore added as he sent a magical force spell down the slope.

Miranda huffed. "Can we hold a cave?"

"As long as there isn't something nasty in the cave," Tufkakes replied, helping Titanya off another Troll.

"There's a cave over there." Titanya pointed down the valley the bears had been in. "It connects to a dungeon we haven't finished yet."

"And might not be populated…" Bigdaddybear grinned. "I like this idea. Horc?"

As he got off a Multiple round of arrows, Horc nodded. It sounded like a good idea to help save everyone. They'd come too far to be stopped by mobs that were lower than they were. They still had people to save. "Run for it."

"Let's go." Bigdaddybear started casting a spell that glowed brown around his hands.

Horc fired more arrows as Bigdaddybear slammed his hands down on the rocky top of the hill. Magic surged out from him where his hands touched the ground. The hill bucked like a wild horse.

Even though Horc struggled to keep his balance, he somehow managed to do it. Most of the others did too, but as he turned to rush down the backside of the hill, he noticed Theodore helping Miranda back to her feet. She looked confused. Horc shook his head as he charged toward their goal with Wolf at his side. She shouldn't be there with them. He was worried that she was going to get more of them killed with her incompetence. He hoped he was wrong.

"What was that spell?" he asked Bigdaddybear as they ran toward the cave at the far side of the valley the bears and other animals had been in.

"Earthquake," Bigdaddybear replied. "Not something I can do very often. The cooldown time is a bitch. Nearly ten minutes. I figured now was a good time to use it. Plus Trolls are more easily knocked off their feet than bears and other four-leggeds are."

Horc jumped over a rock to keep from going around it. "Makes sense."

By the time they reached the cave, they were all breathing hard again.

Sliding to a stop just inside the cave mouth, Horc turned and looked back across the valley. The Ice Trolls were still following them.

"Tufkakes, Jamica, if you could please scout ahead." Horc readied his next arrow. "Casters, let's defend the cave."

"Be back in a few." Tufkakes said, and the two of them disappeared into the shadows.

As the Trolls got close enough, Horc shot the closest one in its light gray eye, flipping its pale blue head back and dropping it. There was still no notification of a critical hit, but the Troll dissolved into pixels before it hit the tundra.

"Is it just me, or are these things getting higher levels as we watch?" Baladara asked as she cast her spells.

"You're right," Titanya stood near Horc with her massive sword out; ready to defend the casters if any of the Trolls got through their barrage. "That one Horc just killed went from level thirty to thirty seven while I had it targeted."

"That's got to be the AI acting up," Stanoran said from the other side. He bounced his massive mace in his hand. "It ain't fair."

"We didn't program the AI to do things like that," Miranda said as she threw one of her trap spells out into the mob heading toward them. The thing exploded and knocked a bunch of them to the ground, but none of them died.

"In case you haven't figured it out yet, the AI has grown beyond the basic programming here." Bigdaddybear cast another wind spell that sent some of the trolls rolling back from the cave. "We can wait to figure out exactly why until we've got the hostages out of the game and safe."

Horc couldn't have put it better himself. He got off several arrows as the Trolls closed in on them.

"Fall back a little farther." Tufkakes appeared out of the shadows. "There's a bottleneck back here. About two people wide. It'll be easy to hold while people go deeper into the cave."

"I like easier to hold." Horc send another Multiple attack flying, then started backing up in the cave. At his side, Baladara got off more spells, even as her group avatar showed her mana dropping to the red.

"Drink this," Bigdaddybear forced a vial into Baladara's hands as they turned and dashed deeper into the cave.

"Light!" Horc hollered as they lost the ambient light coming from the cave mouth.

Tufkakes chuckled. "Sorry. Forgot about that. When we're Shadowwalking, we don't need light."

"Here." Baladara's hands glowed white, then a ball of light appeared above her head and floated about three feet higher than the top of her golden hair.

"Back of the party." Horc held out his hand for her to stop. "We don't need you blinding everyone."

"Ah, good point." Baladara stopped for a second, until everyone was past her. The glow of her light was bright enough to reach several feet in front of Horc as he followed Tufkakes into the cave.

They didn't go very far before Tufkakes stopped and Jamica appeared out of the shadows. They were in a narrow passage that was sufficiently wide for two people to walk side by side, unless either one of them was on the broadside. With Titanya's armored shoulders, no one could be next to her. A knot formed in Horc's throat as he thought that with Rambull's horns, no one would've been striding along with the Shaman either, if he had been still with them. The passage was a good twenty or thirty feet in length.

"We should be able to hold this with three people," Jamica suggested. "The rest could go on and see if the tunnels connect with the AI's lair. If it does, then let us know and we'll come join you."

"We? So you're offering to stay here?" Horc asked.

Jamica nodded. "Although it would make sense to leave several tanks here, we don't have that option. I can use the shadows to my advantage and strike them from behind." A wicked grin crossed her light blue lips. "The others can stop them here. They won't know what hit them."

"Who else wants to stay here and guard our backs?" Horc didn't want to ask people to stay, but was prepared to do so if he needed to.

"I will." Theodore held up his hand. "I feel a bit redundant with Bigdaddybear in the group. He's been with you guys a while. Take him. I'll stay here."

"And so will I." Stanoran pulled his mace and sighed. "If we don't make it out of this, thanks for letting me into the guild, Alan. You've been treating me like a good guy, like a real person. I appreciate that."

Horc gave Stanoran a grin and patted him on the shoulder. "We got off to a rough start in game. I know you're a decent person IRL. You're trying to save your friends too. That means a lot." Somehow Stanoran's word hit Horc harder than he'd expected from any of their previous contact. Maybe their adventure was helping the obnoxious mailroom guy to grow up a little bit.

"Here." Bigdaddybear thrust a bag to Theodore. "Half of the mana potions. Use them as you need them. You've got healers, but you'll need the mana."

Theodore nodded. "Thanks, man. Appreciate it. If we make it through these Ice Trolls, we'll come to give you guys a hand."

"We'll appreciate that." Horc looked at Miranda, Tufkakes, Baladara, and Bigdaddybear.

"I hear them coming," Jamica said, then vanished into the shadows.

"I'll keep scouting ahead." Tufkakes did the same move, fading from view.

"Where do you guys want me to leave you a light?" Baladara said as her hands began glowing white.

Stanoran glanced around. "Over one of us, or on the wall there."

"You'll be the light of the party, Stanoran." Baladara cast the spell and a ball of light appeared over Stanoran. It was the twin to the one over her head.

Horc pointed down the tunnel. "Let's get moving. Good luck guys." He hated splitting the party again, and hoped it wasn't going to be too long. There was a finite number of Ice Trolls, unless the AI was making more on the fly. Eventually they had to run out, and the three would be able to follow them.

As the sounds of battle reached them, Horc and company picked up their pace to a fast jog without any communication between them. Horc hoped the cave would wind around and lead them in the direction they needed to go to find the hostages and defeat the dragon. According to the arrow, they were heading parallel to the direction they needed to go. At least they weren't heading away from it.

16

THE TUNNEL wound around. Horc had to force himself to pay attention to where they were going and not watch the others' icons in his view. Their health and mana went up and down as they fought, drank potions, and struggled to guard the party's rear.

"We just have to tell ourselves that they're going to be fine," Baladara said as they rounded a corner.

Horc frowned. "I know. I hate splitting the party like this. It doesn't end well."

"Maybe this time will be different," Tufkakes said. "If we're successful and knock the AI out, we'll all be safe and sound back in our pods."

They rounded a curve and everyone came to a stop. Ahead of them was a vast cavern full of multicolored crystals, many of them larger around than Horc was. They were all different colors and when the light from Baladara's spell hit them, it fractured and created rainbows in hues Horc had never seen before.

"Wow." Horc stared at the beauty of it all.

"This isn't right." Miranda shook her head, then looked like she was accessing something on her screen. "Yeah, definitely not right. This shouldn't be here. None of this should. I was giving allowances for the tunnel, but this crystal cavern. No way."

"Do you think the AI did this?" Bigdaddybear asked as he walked over and ran a hand over one of the crystals. "They feel real enough."

Miranda walked over and tapped one. A soft chime rang out in the cavern. "If the AI did this, it's continuing to reach beyond its base programming. It wasn't supposed to be creating environments. Well outside of things like making it rain or snow in certain areas."

Horc walked over to one of the huge crystals that was in a shade of dark blue he'd never seen in the real world before. It was almost like someone had taken the color of the ocean and merged it with a twilight sky. He was surprised it was solid and not liquid. "It was building a wall around the arena. Isn't that creating an environment?"

"I think I understand what she's getting at," Bigdaddybear said. "That was a manipulation of an environment, adding buildings and walls is something a human would do."

"But to build a crystal cavern…" Tufkakes looked around and his voice trailed off for a second.

"That would take a god," Titanya finished for him. "Wow. This AI is full of itself, isn't it?"

"That's one way to put it." Horc stepped away from the dark blue crystal. "Let's keep moving so we can shut this thing down." With Wolf at his side, he headed down the curving path covered in small crystal shards that pricked at his boots.

After a minute Baladara stopped and glared down at the trail as she shook her foot, like she was trying to get pain to go away. "This isn't cool." She looked back at Bigdaddybear. "This isn't in my mage spell book. Do you have anything?"

Bigdaddybear got the faraway look they all got when they were accessing their gaming data. After a moment, he pursed his lips and huffed. "Maybe. It takes a lot of heat to melt crystals, depending on what they're made of. We don't know what these things are. And we're in a cavern. This could be a major mistake."

"Or it could make our going easier." Tufkakes leaned against one of the crystals and pulled off his boot to rub his foot.

"Worth the chance," Horc agreed. He hadn't had one of the crystals make it all the way through the leather soles of his boots to go through his socks and into his skin, but he didn't want it to reach that point. He glanced over where Wolf was sitting, licking his bleeding paws. There had to be something he could do to make his companion more comfortable, but he didn't know what people IRL did for hot sidewalks or rough rocks to make it easier for their dogs.

Bigdaddybear nodded and without another word, started the spell. His hands glowed brown, the slowly changed to red as he worked the magic. When he thrust his paw-like hands out, energy rippled off them.

For a second it felt like nothing was going to happen. Then the cavern began to shake. Crystals tinkled. The refracted light from Baladara's spell danced through the crystals.

A gust of warm air started light and built up intensity as the chamber rocked.

"An earthquake?" Horc muttered. "I don't think an earthquake was a good idea." He shifted to a wide stance in an effort to keep his balance and remain standing.

"It's not a quake." Bigdaddybear corrected him. "It's supposed to be a Volcanic Earth spell. It's supposed to make the ground molten for a few seconds."

The crystals began rocking hard, some of them cracking and splintering as they crashed to the ground around the party.

Titanya lifted her shield over her head and looked braced for impact.

"I've got this," Baladara said and cast a shield around them.

"You know if you just brought this cavern down around our ears, you're not as smart as you think you are," Miranda said, gripping her club and looking worried.

Horc didn't want to get insulting, be he was thinking it might've been a better idea to not just try out a new spell in a situation where unforeseen effects might get them all killed. The way the cavern was shifting around them, he wasn't sure any of the beautiful crystals would be left when the spell was over.

Then the heat multiplied a thousandfold. Horc gasped for breath and reached into his pack for a canteen. His health flashed and began to drop.

The floor of the cavern glowed and bubbled.

"Not good, big guy," Tufkakes said. "This AOE is hitting us too."

Everyone's health bars were dropping as Horc looked at the icons on his screen. It wasn't massive drops, but it was so much that if they had been lower level toons, they'd be in trouble fast. He hoped the spell wouldn't go on too long; that would also be bad.

Then as subtly as it had started, the rumbling and shaking stopped.

Horc's health had only taken about a ten percent drop. He let out the breath he'd been holding.

Baladara glared at Bigdaddybear. "Okay. Is it done?"

Bigdaddybear nodded, then pointed to the ground. "Done and it worked."

"Good." Baladara dropped her spell and a few more small crystals fell down on the party. They'd obviously been sitting on top of the shield.

There was a ring of more crystals laying around the edge of the shield. In spots they formed a short wall about two feet tall. Lying on the cavern floor like that, they looked more like pretty rocks than crystals. Just beyond the wall, the floor of the cavern gleamed, looking like a highly polished stone floor. As Horc watched, a few last molten bubbles rose up, popped and then the floor stopped moving.

Titanya went to the edge of the area that had been protected by the magical shield, bent over and tapped the path with the tip of her sword. "Seems solid enough."

"Definitely." Tufkakes did a graceful jump above the wall and then rolled across the floor until he ended up against one of the crystals that had fallen.

Taking it as everything was going to be fine, Horc stepped over the short wall. "Good, then let's get moving."

Something scratched against a crystal not far away from him. He stopped walking and stared toward the sound.

Wolf growled a warning.

"Now what?" Baladara asked just as a swarm of clear spiders scampered over the crystals and rushed them.

"You had to ask, didn't you?" Tufkakes said and started tossing knives at the arachnids that were slightly larger than some of the wolf spiders Horc used to find IRL.

The knives impaled the spiders, but there were a lot more of the almost crystal-clear arachnids than Tufkakes had knives.

Horc pulled his bow from his shoulder and started hitting spiders with arrows.

Baladara yelped and the spell she'd been about to cast fizzled in her hands as she yanked a spider off her skirt and hurled it toward the nearest crystal. "AOE people, AOE. Single attacks aren't going to help us much."

"Working on it." Bigdaddybear's hands glowed almost white right before lightning erupted around them.

The electrical assault knocked some of the spiders back and fried others.

Horc tossed a Fire Pit Trap out. Almost instantly, the trap went off, incinerating a group of bugs, but more kept coming, pausing at the edge of the flaming pit to form a living chain of spiders to get across the pit.

"Yeah, this isn't good." Miranda swung her club, and a swath of flame shot out of the tip of it, taking out the spiders who made it across the pit.

Titanya frowned at her. "What's with that club of yours? Doesn't look like standard issue."

Miranda shrugged. "I'm one of the support staff, why should I have standard issue anything?"

"To put you on the same level as the rest of us," Horc said as he threw out an Explosive Trap at the same time Baladara managed to get an AOE fire spell off. It irritated him that Miranda had set herself up as better than the rest of them just because she could. Sure it was a rescue job and they needed every option they could, but it set off his personal sensibilities. He hated overpowered characters, and Miranda had created herself to be just that. After she'd interfered with the Gnoll King kill, she'd pissed him off, but now she was really working his nerves. Of course, it made things easier, but it took some of the fun of the game away. He had to keep telling himself that she was useful and not just a buzz-kill.

"Not my thing." She shook her head and took out another group of spiders.

"We need to try to keep moving," Titanya said as she did some kind of blast spell by striking the ground hard with her sword. Concussive force rolled out from her, bowling spiders back from the path.

"Good point." Horc pointed toward her. "Let's form up and keep going. Hopefully these things won't chase us too far."

Baladara let out a laugh as she did another large area of fire. "Like those damned Trolls didn't agro train the hell out of us."

"If we can get through the cavern, I think I may have an idea," Bigdaddybear said as he sent a swarm rolling away from them in a magical gust of wind.

"It won't work now?" Horc asked as he loosed a Multiple Shot barrage before starting his next trap spell. He was going through mana like crazy and hoped he wouldn't run out too soon.

Bigdaddybear shook his head as they fell in behind Titanya. "Don't want to risk it here, we might end up trapped."

If it hadn't been for the spiders and the crystals they had destroyed, Horc could think of uglier places to be trapped, but that didn't really matter. They didn't have time to get trapped somewhere. They needed to get to the hostages and get everyone free of the game.

They made slow progress, working their way across the cavern with the spiders around them at every step. The second any of them stopped their assaults to get a mana potion, or even take a breath, the spiders came through the hole in their defenses. During those times, Wolf managed to kill his share of spiders, although he tended to bear the brunt of the attack then. Luckily, Horc was there with healing spells for him after the nastier assaults.

Finally, after what felt like hours, they reached the edge of the cavern and the tunnel leading onward. Horc was surprised they were actually going in the direction the map arrow wanted them to go.

"Alright, Bigdaddybear, here's your opportunity." Horc stepped out of the cavern with its floor of molten crystal onto the dirt of the tunnel beyond it.

"Everyone get back. Horc, Baladara, if I could get a couple of explosions to hold them off." Bigdaddybear shook out his hands, then stopped and downed a mana potion. "If things keep up like this, we're going to run out of these." He slipped the vial back into his bag.

Miranda shook her head. "Don't worry. I've got an everfull bottle of both mana and health potions. We'll be fine."

Horc was torn between saying something, and or just rolling his eyes. He opted to keep his mouth shut and tossed a Fire Pit spell out into the narrow spot where the cavern met the tunnel. Seconds later, it went up. Spiders died and then Baladara's spell went off frying the ones on the other side.

"This won't hold them long," Tufkakes said, looking despondently at his bandolier that was missing half of his daggers.

"Doesn't have to." Bigdaddybear started his spell. "Just get ready to take out the stragglers."

Horc had enough mana for a Multiple Shot barrage and he readied it as Bigdaddybear unleashed his spell. Like the volcano spell. Nothing happened at first. Spiders started forming a living chain to get across the pit Horc's trap had left in the floor.

The mountain shook. It was more violent than the volcano spell had been. Try as he might, Horc couldn't maintain his feet as the ground moved under him.

In the cavern, the crystals tremored and shattered. The sound was beautiful at first, then the tones became painful as the crystals broke apart, sending shards flying in all directions. Spiders were impaled on fragments of crystal. Some were crushed under the weight of the huge ones that fell before exploding into glittering shrapnel.

Dirt and dust from the tunnel sifted down on the party as the mountain continued to shimmy and shake.

From the ground next to Horc, Baladara started a spell then shook her head. "I don't have the mana for a shield. Sorry."

"Don't worry." Horc had failed to cast his Multiple Shot barrage when he'd been knocked off his feet, but it didn't matter. There were no spiders rushing toward them any longer. A pair of massive crystals had fallen across the mouth of the tunnel, blocking them off from the way they'd come, and stopping any aggressive mobs from coming at them.

"Looks like we're not going out that way," Miranda said with a frown. "Good work, Bearboy."

"Didn't see you and your magic club coming up with anything better," Bigdaddybear grumbled back.

Although Horc could understand the urge to put the woman in her place, he put a hand on Bigdaddybear's furry shoulder. "Let's get out of here." He nodded on down the tunnel.

Bigdaddybear nodded. "Definitely."

"I'll scout ahead again," Tufkakes said, then melted into the shadows.

They fell back into their normal formation with Titanya in front, as they headed down the tunnel. Although everyone but himself and Baladara had made massive changes to their toons' race and or class, and they had Miranda with them instead of Slasher, Horc flashed back to their adventure in the Gnoll King's dungeon. They'd prowled the levels of that adventure in much the same formation. The dangers there had been just as real, but they'd been a little clumsier as they'd been figuring out what their toons could do. They had most things figured out. But he wasn't sure it was going to be enough, particularly as the AI had figured out how to create whole environments.

17

THE TUNNEL they were in ended at the shore of a huge underground lake. Light from glowing crystals bathed the place in an eerie quiet beauty. The water on the lake was perfectly still. There didn't appear to be anything in the massive cave to stir the water, although the far shore was completely out of sight.

"And now we need another boat," Baladara muttered as they all stood there looking across the surface.

The cave walls reached the edge of the water, at least where they were standing at the edge of the tunnel. There didn't appear to be any way around, or over the lake.

Horc sighed. "I'm not liking the idea of swimming across this lake."

Miranda shrugged. "We don't get tired driving our toons, what's the problem?"

"Haven't you noticed that we do start taking damage when we start over exerting ourselves?" Horc glared at her. As much as he wanted to, the edge of a massive underground lake wasn't the place to have a big fight with the woman.

"Was that what was happening?" Tufkakes asked. "That last fight with the spiders. Even when they weren't hitting and I had no indication of poison, I was still taking damage. I thought the crystals were doing something to me."

Bigdaddybear shook his head. "No. We think it's the AI manipulating game play. It's like the thing is trying to make our toons more human or something."

"Could it be trying to become more human?" Titanya mused. "I know that's more likely to happen in science fiction stories, the robots wanting to be human. But what if something they used to program the thing is making it want to be more like us?"

"That doesn't make any sense," Miranda said with a scoff. "It's superior to humans, why would it want to be more like us?"

"Why would it want to make itself a dragon body and become real in the game?" Horc asked as he waded a short distance into the lake. The ripples he created broke the surface for a while, then faded into the distance. It made him wonder if he was the first thing to ever break the surface of the water. What was the AI planning with something like the lake?

Bigdaddybear waded out next to Horc. "If it's creating things like this lake, has it become real in the game, or is this something it did before getting to that point?"

"Maybe it made the dragon body but is still keeping its fingers in the godlike stuff, like this lake," Tufkakes said, walking out to them. "Guess we really don't have much option than to swim, do we?"

Horc shook his head. "Not if we want to keep going. We can't go back the way we came, there're crystals blocking the way."

Their guild chat beeped.

Guys, I think we finally beat back the Trolls. Stanoran

At least there are no more of them currently coming at us. Theodore

Good. Horc grinned as he replied to their message. Although he'd been monitoring their health and mana as they traversed the tunnel, it was good to hear from the others. *Unfortunately you can't catch up with us, there're some crystals blocking the way. We can't come back that way either.*

Then we'll see about finding another way around. Stanoran

Be careful. It looks like the AI is creating environments now. Horc

Not good. Theodore. *We'll keep our eyes peeled and let you know if we encounter anything else odd.*

Horc waited a minute or two, but nothing else popped up.

"Sounds like the First Responders are being a super-kick-ass guild," Baladara said.

"Yeah." Horc nodded and stared across the quiet lake. He wished they could see the far side of it. That would make him feel better about it, or at the very least give them a goal to shoot for. "Okay, so I guess we should break down and swim for it."

"I was afraid you were going to say that," Miranda muttered before wading out toward them.

"At least you're not the one covered in fur," Tufkakes replied. "I hope our packs are waterproof."

That was something Horc hadn't even thought about, but figured the magic of the packs would help keep their stuff safe as they swam. They hadn't noticed any damage to things after their fight with the sea monster. He pulled his bow off his shoulder and slipped it into the pack, something he wouldn't be able to do IRL with most bows and most packs. Then he pulled his dagger out of his belt and did the same before repeating the maneuver with his quiver. When he turned his attention back to the lake, the others had done the same with their weapons. Titanya also took off her armor and added it to her pack. Seeing her do that made Horc thankful their bags were magical and didn't add weight to the players no matter how much was put in. As long as they didn't fill up all their bag slots they'd be fine.

Wolf stood quietly at Horc's side, looking out across the lake.

With a heavy sigh, Horc resumed wading out into the water, thankful it wasn't ice cold like he expected, but somewhere shy of comfortably warm. He walked as long as he could. Wolf was the first one of them to start swimming. Baladara followed him. As Horc lay across the water and started swimming without really thinking about the action, he wondered if some of the guild who'd been lost, Scarletcrest and Rambull would've been able to swim. The Minotauren seemed too big and bulky to do it easily, although the Gnome might've done it with no problem, he'd have had to do it for longer than the larger Humans, Elves, and Ursans would've had to.

Keeping the cave walls on either side of them as long as he could since the distance seemed to get greater as they swam along, Horc did his best to keep everyone moving the direction the tunnel had been leading them. The arrow on his mini map was helping him more with that than it had any time since they entered the tunnels.

HORC WASN'T sure how long they'd been swimming. His arms and legs were starting to burn. None of the others were complaining, but when he glanced at the group icons, it was obvious Baladara and Miranda were starting to have trouble. Both of them were starting to lose health and there wasn't anything attacking them except for the water, and it wasn't doing anything but sliding away under them with each stroke of their arms.

"Can everyone stop and tread water for a moment?" Horc pulled up and lifted his head clear of the water.

Around him, the others did the same.

"You know, it's a good thing our toons innately know how to do things like this," Titanya said. "Swimming has never been my strong point."

"I hear you," Horc agreed. "Some of us are starting to show signs of fatigue. Bigdaddybear, can you please hit everyone with a round of healing? Then get a mana potion. I doubt we can eat while swimming."

"Health potions work," Tufkakes said. "I used one a few minutes ago when I noticed my health dropping. Thought it would be a good idea to stay maxed out in case we have something hit us when we're not looking."

"Good thinking." Horc's arms burned more from the treading water, even though he wasn't putting as much effort into it as he had swimming.

"Yeah, give me a second, and I'll hit all of us." Bigdaddybear's hands started their blue glow. "I keep hoping we'll hit the end of this thing soon."

"Me too." Horc glanced around and fought back a slight wave of panic. He couldn't see the cave walls, and the ceiling seemed to be closer than it had when they started out. The crystals that were still providing light looked almost close enough to touch. If they hadn't been in the water, most of them would've been stooping to avoid hitting the crystals. He wanted to keep moving and reach the far side of the lake. Logic demanded that the lake had to end at some point, it couldn't just keep going and going and going.

The warmth of Bigdaddybear's healing spell swept over Horc and the burning in his arms and legs stopped. He felt like he was ready to swim the rest of the way, no matter how far it was. "Thanks."

Bigdaddybear smiled and nodded. "No problem. That's why you keep healers in the party, right?"

"Definitely," Tufkakes said before Horc could. "Now let's keep going. I'm ready to get my fur dry."

"Me too." Bigdaddybear accepted the potion Baladara handed him and downed it quickly before putting the vial in his pack.

Horc lay across the water again and resumed his easy strokes toward the distant shore. He told himself the shore was there, they weren't going to just swim and swim until they ran out of mana potions and Bigdaddybear couldn't heal them anymore. Since they'd given half of their potions to the rest of the party, that might happen sooner rather than later. Horc wasn't keen on asking Miranda for her unlimited supply. It felt too much like cheating, even if the AI was already cheating.

"HEY, IS that what I think it is?" Baladara paused and pointed while treading water.

Horc pulled up alongside her and followed her finger. It looked like a cave wall ahead of them. He couldn't tell how far, but seeing it there encouraged him. "Looks that way."

"Good." Tufkakes huffed. "Maybe we can all hold out until we get there and then collapse on the beach. Now if we just had some sun and surf, I could pretend we were on Padre and take a well-deserved nap."

Baladara laughed, it was the first cheerful sound out of the group since they entered the water. "I'm with you there. Maybe when we get out of this game we can go hang out on the beach for a month and recuperate." She sighed. "I think when I get to the beach, I'm passing things over to Lisa for a bit so I can go take a nap. Who knew swimming was such a pain in the ass?"

"You deserve it," Horc said as he pushed himself toward the distant shore. He couldn't recall when Mike took back over Baladara, after recovering from the spell feed back, but the two had to keep working together to keep ahead of the real-world fatigue that hit them from using gloves and goggles."We all do."

Bigdaddybear swam next to him. "It might be a good idea for us to take a rest when we get to the shore. If it looks safe, we can leave Lisa to watch over us."

"I should be able to help with that too," Miranda said. "I made sure to give myself max stamina, so I'll be good longer than you guys will."

Horc nodded slowly. "Of course you did. Sure that sounds like a great plan."

Then they were all swimming again, and they weren't able to continue talking.

As the shore drew closer, Horc thought about just telling Mike to log out and let them finish up the rescue, but he knew his friend wouldn't do that. They were all in the game together. They would all see it to the end or die trying and not be able to log back in and help finish off the AI. They were living up to the name they'd chosen for the guild. First Responders didn't stop until everyone was safe. The energy the others were giving their efforts to get to shore and continue their quest pushed Horc on.

18

HORC SANK to his knees when he reached the beach. He couldn't remember the last time he had been so tired. His health was down to below half, but they'd been determined to get to shore and not ask Bigdaddybear for more healing, hoping they could get some rest and recover their hit points naturally.

"AH GUYS, I think there's something coming," Miranda sounded almost scared as Horc came awake with a start at her voice.

Horc glanced around. They were still on the beach of the massive underground lake. Light still radiated out from the numerous crystals in the ceiling. Around him, the rest of the party jerked awake.

"Where?" Horc looked around but couldn't see anything coming down the tunnel they had slept near.

"Over there." Baladara pointed out into the lake.

Horc stared out across the lake. Ripples danced across the water as something swam toward them. He glanced at his and everyone else's health bars. They were all full, as was everyone's mana. They were ready to renew their battle with the AI.

"Okay, how come there's something in the lake now and there wasn't earlier?" Tufkakes pulled his bandolier out of his pack and slung it across his chest before pulling out a pair of daggers.

"No clue." Titanya replied as she scrambled to get her armor on and her weapon out.

Bigdaddybear frowned. "This isn't good. I sent Rick a message as we were getting comfortable on the beach and so far there hasn't been a response."

"Do you think you can focus on the situation at hand?" Miranda snapped. "We'll worry about the outside world later."

"It's not here yet." Horc stared as hard as he could toward the wake that was coming at them. He couldn't make out anything in the water, and from the width of the waves, it looked to be made by something rather large. "Our connection to the outside has been important." He didn't want to feel like they'd been cut off. Being trapped with no way to reach out for help would make the situation that much more dire.

"She's right." Bigdaddybear set his jaw, looking grim. "We have to focus on the here and now. I just sent another message, just in case there was a technical hiccup with the previous one."

"Okay." Horc pulled his bow out of his pack, and then slung his quiver over his shoulder. He felt better with weapons in his hand and at the ready.

"Ah man, why does this look like something out of a Godzilla movie?" Tufkakes asked as he backed up a couple of steps.

The water rippled and a huge, green, smooth head appeared out of the water. It was broad with large bulbous eyes that looked a lot like a frog, if a frog had a head that was six feet across. It didn't hop out of the water, so much as wade rapidly. It had humanoid shoulders and body with webbed hands. The water sliding off its body made it look slimy as it rushed toward them.

The red text above its head said **Friggispiran, level 50** with three stars next to it.

"What is that?" Miranda shouted as she swung her club and shot flame at it.

"No clue," Horc replied as he unleashed a Flaming razor arrow. The Friggispiran was easily the most powerful thing they'd faced in Halfworld. Everyone got in solid hits on it before Wolf reached it. Their attacks only dropped its health a little bit, not as much as Horc would've liked. Particularly since they weren't getting any XP for any of the monsters they were fighting, he didn't like major fights. If the AI hadn't screwed with things, he'd have reveled in the major battle, but he wanted to get done and rescue people before things turned nasty.

The Friggispiran make a sound that was a lot like a cat heaving up a hairball. Seconds later it spat a huge ball of slime green goo at Titanya. She tried to dodge out of the way, then at the last second brought her massive manga sword around and sliced the goo ball in half. It didn't slow down the slimy attack, but it did lesson the amount of it that splashed on her armor.

Where the ball struck, smoke instantly started billowing up from her shiny protections.

"Get in the water!" Bigdaddybear shouted. "Try to wash it off."

"Great, not only is it a giant toad of some-sort, but it spits acid," Tufkakes said as he threw two knives at the thing, catching it in the throat. The drop in its HP was barely noticeable on its health bar.

Horc got off an impact arrow. "Then let's take it down quickly."

Steam rolled up out of the water as Titanya rushed in and tried to get the goo off her armor.

Bigdaddybear launched a spell at the Friggispiran, turning the ground under it to mud that the great toad-like creature mired in. Seconds later, the beach sand re-solidified and the Friggispiran was slowed down even farther as it struggled to get free of its gritty prison.

Horc threw a trap at the Friggispiran, placing it between the beast and the party. It continued to fight to get out of the sand.

"Water's not helping!" Titanya shouted as she rushed back toward the shore, her armor still smoking, leaving steam trailing behind her as she tore at the straps of the armor to get it off.

"Let me help." Tufkakes hurried over to her and began aiding her in getting out of the armor as Horc, Baladara, Wolf, Bigdaddybear, and Miranda continued their assault on the thing.

With a yelp, Wolf went flying over their heads and crashed into the cave wall after the thing stopped trying to get out of the sand, and grabbed hold of him to throw him away.

"This abomination shouldn't exist," Miranda said as she rushed forward and actually hit it with her club. The physical blow finally dropped the thing to just under three quarters health.

"It appears to be more resistant to magic," Bigdaddybear shouted. "We need to be more direct with it."

The Friggispiran batted Miranda away and somehow managed to free itself from the sand holding it down. It stumbled slightly and landed a foot in Horc's Flaming Pit Trap. The damage from the magical instant hole wasn't nearly as much as Miranda's club attack had been.

"Then let's do that." Baladara finished the spell she'd started, then as the Friggispiran caught fire, clutched her staff and charged forward.

Horc wasn't sure he liked the idea of getting close to the thing, so he stopped worrying about magical buffs to his arrows and stuck with basic shots to hit it as hard as he could from a distance.

Titanya got her smoking armor off and left the pieces smoldering in the sand. In just her tunic and armored pants, she picked up her massive sword and rushed the Friggispiran.

Close melee did a lot more damage to the thing, and they kept it up, with even Tufkakes getting in and hitting it hard and fast. Horc would've closed ranks if he had still had a hand-held weapon that could do as much damage as his arrows.

For several minutes they fought with the Friggispiran who tried grabbing them and throwing them away like it had Wolf. Bigdaddybear was nimble enough to avoid the attacks. Baladara managed to cast a floating spell of some sort each time she went flying so her damage was minimal. Miranda suffered the most from the blows. Titanya always met the grabs with blocks from her sword, sending the Friggispiran back a couple of steps.

"Guys, we've got something else heading this way." Tufkakes pointed out to the lake.

Horc frowned at the sight of the new wake making a line straight for shore. He pulled out an impact arrow. The first one he'd tried had at least slowed the Friggispiran down, even if it hadn't done much damage to the thing. "Hit it hard and fast when it slows down. We need to take this thing down and make a run for it." The idea that the AI was generating giant frog beasts to keep them from their objectives pissed him off. He fired the arrow, catching the Friggispiran in one bulbous eye.

The damage was impressive, even if it didn't flash critical strike on his screen. The Friggispiran roared and spat another glob of acid goo, this time toward Horc.

Jumping out of the way. Horc fired another arrow as the goo hit the sand and instantly started smoking. The smoke was thick enough to quickly obscur his view of the beast, although the sounds of his party beating on it continued to be loud.

On his screen, the Friggispiran's health was flashing orange. Horc fired arrows as quickly as he could at where he'd last seen the thing.

"This smoke is getting obnoxious," Baladara shouted, then coughed.

"Noxious is more like it." Bigdaddybear replied. Then a wind whipped up and started blowing it away.

"Don't worry about the smoke." Horc kept firing arrows, thankful for his ever-full quiver. "Let's get this thing down and make a run for it before the other one gets here."

"Definitely." Tufkakes appeared out of the smoke and hit the thing from behind. Again, there was no sign of a critical hit, but its health dropped into the red and it roared in pain. Suddenly the Friggispiran turned and headed back into the lake.

"Oh no you don't." Titanya sliced it through the legs. The thing was low enough for her to manage to sever the legs just above the knees. The Friggispiran flopped to the ground as Miranda landed a blow with her club, sending the thing into pixels.

"Let's run!" Horc shouted and spun toward the tunnel. He didn't want to face another of the monsters and be slowed down again.

Titanya was down under half health, as was Miranda. Tufkakes had taken a fair amount of damage and Wolf was in need of healing.

"Once we're clear, we need to pause so I can heal people," Bigdaddybear said as they entered the tunnel, heading in the direction of the arrow that was leading them toward the AI dragon and its hostages.

"I want to make sure we don't get jumped by another of those things." Horc said as they followed the tunnel around a turn. He wanted the party at full strength too, but they couldn't handle more delays.

They had to put some distance between them and the lake. Had their rest on the shores had given the AI time to come up with the Friggispiran attack plan? If it had needed time to plan, that gave them a chance if they could move faster and get to it before it came up with a way to block them from getting to the hostages.

19

HORC HUFFED hard as they rounded the fourth turn in the tunnel. He figured they had to be a good mile or more away from the underground lake.

"Everyone be quiet for a moment," Tufkakes said, holding up a hand. "Stop breathing."

Not sure what he was on about, Horc did as he asked. His chest was already sore from the run; he hoped Tufkakes had a good reason.

After a second, Tufkakes nodded. "I don't hear anything running after us. All quiet."

Horc let out the breath. "Good." He was really tired of running, swimming and otherwise fleeing nearly everything they were running into in the tunnel.

Beside him, Wolf's head hung low and his tongue nearly hit the tunnel floor. Horc glanced at his companion's health and it looked okay, but he had no idea if the new rules about exhaustion impacted Wolf as it was everyone else. For good measure, Horc tossed him a chunk of meat. His supply was starting to get low. Not getting loot was impacting that.

Titanya pulled off her pack and began rummaging through it. "It's a step or two down from what I was wearing, but I've got backup armor."

Baladara stared at her. "Who carries backup armor?"

"Someone who's prepared," Titanya replied as she started pulling pieces of armor from her pack. "I always carry a backup set, normally the last armor I wore before I found something nicer. I know it sounds silly, but this time it's coming in handy."

Bigdaddybear nodded. "I understand. I've done things like that in other games."

Since he wasn't used to personal armor in the science fiction games he'd played before Halfworld, it sounded like a bad use of bag space, under normal circumstances. Since they were dealing with not getting loot, or being able to safely visit vendors, it made lots of sense for their current conditions. If he'd been thinking along those lines, he'd have kept a backup melee weapon and would be able to help the party more.

When she was done putting her armor on, Titanya thumped her chest. "Yeah, that's better. I was almost naked without my armor. I couldn't be a good tank in that condition."

"And we need a good tank," Baladara said.

"Let's keep moving." Although Horc was thankful for the down time while Titanya got re-armored, he wanted to continue toward their quest. The arrow was almost straight down the tunnel.

Tufkakes came back from slightly down the tunnel. "Yeah, now's a good time."

Horc blinked at their Rogue. "Why? Did you hear that thing chasing us?" The way their luck was running, it would be getting close and they'd have to take off running again.

"Not sure." Tufkakes shrugged. "But if it does come charging after us, it's going to be in for a nasty surprise when it comes down the tunnel and hits the traps I just laid. Since they aren't magical, we don't have to worry about them fading away."

"Let's just hope we don't have to come back out this way," Miranda muttered.

"Considering those crystals between us and the outside," Horc was getting really tired of her attitude, which seemed to be getting worse the farther into the tunnels they went, "yeah, I hope we don't have to come back this way. At that point, it might just be easier to log out of the game." He wasn't about to do that until he had everyone safe, and he figured they all knew that. If it came to having to turn back, they'd do everything they could to find an alternate course through the tunnels in hope of finding clear passage.

Horc headed on down the way they'd been going.

Tufkakes jogged ahead of him. "I'll take point." Then he faded into the shadows.

Having the Rogue out front made Horc feel better, although deep in his gut he still felt like he should be the one scouting ahead. He was the ranger after all.

A FEW minutes later, Tufkakes was waiting for them, leaning calmly on the passage wall. "We've got a bit of a decision to make here."

Since the tunnel had been non-branching, Horc had a sinking feeling he knew what they were about to be asked. "How many?"

"Just a fork." Tufkakes replied. "I went down both sides for short distances. They're running the same direction as far as north south go, but one slopes up and the other slopes down."

"Well, that's different." Baladara glanced at Miranda. "I'm guessing this isn't on that up-to-date map of yours."

Miranda rolled her eyes. "You know my map hasn't been accurate since we split with the rest of the party."

Horc rubbed the bridge of his nose. "Yes, we know. Any suggestions on which way we should go?" It was probably too much to ask for things to lead them straight to the hostages.

For nearly half a minute, everything was silent, then everyone spoke at once.

"Up," Baladara said. "Makes more sense than down."

"Down," Bigdaddybear replied. "Probably the deeper the better."

"Up." Titanya threw in without additional commentary.

"If the AI dragon is flying people in, up makes more sense." Tufkakes was somehow louder than the rest.

"Down, we have to go down," Miranda insisted.

Horc sighed and held up his hand for silence. "Wasn't expecting everyone to go at once." He glanced down at Wolf. "Do you have an opinion?"

Wolf looked at him, then wandered over to the left hand fork.

Horc looked at Tufkakes. "Which one is that?"

Tufkakes grinned. "Up."

"Four to two with me abstaining is a clear majority." Horc walked over the upward-slopping passage. "So we go up."

"Why does the pet get a vote?" Miranda asked. "He's not even a real person."

Reaching down to scratch Wolf's ears, Horc glared at her. "You know, he might just be bits of code and light…or whatever things are made of in this game, but he's been better to me than a lot of the players, who are people I work with every day. I'm the guild leader here, and I say he gets a vote if he wants one."

Wolf licked his hand.

Miranda put her hands on her hips and matched his glare. "And what if the AI is controlling him, using your companion to watch our every move?"

It was a question that had never crossed his mind. He was so used to having Wolf at his side, even before the AI went nuts and started trying to control everything about the game. He'd had to plead with the Ranger trainer to get to keep Wolf when he finished his companion quests. Wolf didn't act like the other NPCs in the game, he was more like one of the party… no, not like one of the party, he was one of the party. Being bound to Horc had to make him different. There was no way the AI was using Wolf against him.

Horc shook his head. "I won't believe that of him. He's not shown any signs of not being one of us." He squatted down next to Wolf and gave him a brief hug, and Wolf licked his face.

Setting his jaw, Horc stood and started off down the new tunnel, determined to prove Miranda wrong. Wolf was part of the party and his friend.

20

HORC RUBBED his arms. The path had leveled out for a while, but it was getting colder. The quest arrow was still pointing them in the direction the tunnel ran, and again there hadn't been any more branching. It was starting to feel too easy, and that made him nervous.

A loud, squawking bray came from ahead just as Tufkakes came running back. "Slow down guys, we've got trouble." He skidded to a stop and wiped his hand across his forehead, making Horc wonder if Procyans could sweat under all that fur.

"What's wrong?" Titanya drew her sword and stared past Tufkakes.

"Giant, man-eating, or in my case, raccoon-eating, penguins." Tufkakes glanced back over his shoulder. "At least they can't fly and aren't that fast on land." The squawking brays continued from the tunnel.

"Any way around them?" Horc asked, knocking an arrow.

"If they hadn't all come swarming out of their little side passage, maybe, but they're following me." Tufkakes turned back the way he'd come. "This might get messy."

"Wait a minute," Baladara interrupted as she started the motions to cast her spell. "When you left, you were Shadowwalking. What happened?"

Tufkakes pulled a couple of daggers. "Not sure. Maybe those things have sonar or something."

"More real-world adaptations for in-game mobs." Bigdaddybear rubbed his chin. "The AI is getting way too creative."

Tufkakes shook his head. "The giant goo-spitting frog man was creative, these things just ain't right."

"And they're being vocal," Miranda said, holding her club at the ready. "So far, most of the mobs haven't been vocal. The AI is advancing, maybe even getting more scientific."

"Scientific?" Tufkakes frowned at her. "Wait until you see them, and then decide how factual they are."

The cacophony got closer, then the first wave of them rushed toward the party. The red text above them said **Piranahquins, level 49**. They were nearly man sized, looked like emperor penguins but with huge fang like teeth filling their long beaks. Physically, it didn't make any sense whatsoever. As they ran, they flapped their flippers and continued their braying.

"Ah geez, just shut up already." Baladara unleashed a Fireball at the first one.

Horc followed up with a Fire razor arrow.

The flaming piranahquin flew backwards, knocking several of the other ones over as it went.

"Well that was something I don't think I ever wanted to see—" Bigdaddybear flung a Wind spell at them, bowling more over— "flaming flying piranhaquins."

"Don't say that three times fast," Titanya said before she leveled her sword and charged into the fray.

"This makes no sense," Miranda muttered as she swung her club and sent a jet of fire toward the oncoming mob. "It shouldn't be making up its own creatures. Particularly not things like this. It's almost like someone has plugged it into the internet and it's just-"

"Downloading anything and everything it can get its hands on." Horc interrupted as he fired more arrows at it.

All of a sudden everything was making sense. The programmers had taught the AI how to learn, but they hadn't taught it how to tell the difference between real and imaginary, it also didn't know the difference between right and wrong. The problem was, with everything coming at them non-stop, he had no idea how they were going to combat that point of its training. He needed time to think, or better yet, find a way to get back in touch with Rick and the other programmers outside the game.

A piranhaquin broke through the mass of them caught in the wind and fire. It rushed forward. Horc turned his attention to it. Even as he hit it with arrows, he was amazed how much like the emperor penguins at the aquarium it looked. There weren't many left in the wild due to the Antarctic ice melting and destroying their habitat, but he'd seen them and several other species at the Dallas World Aquarium that had been expanding to help more people understand the life forms they were losing to climate change and habitat destruction. The way the black and white feathers were patterned, the things were nearly identical to the flightless birds, but no birds had teeth in their bills. The only time he could remember seeing that was in some photo manipulations when he was a kid.

Wolf jumped the piranhaquin charging Horc and bore it down to the ground. Horc caught it with two more arrows and it lay still.

"At least they're going down easier than that damned frog thing," Baladara said as she got off another Fireball.

"They aren't specials," Bigdaddybear replied. "No stars next to their names."

"But there's a lot of them." Horc found his next target as it came out of the pack and started toward them.

"That there are," Baladara agreed.

When this attacker was down, Horc tossed a couple of trap spells into the middle of the piranhaquins, they went off quickly, making feathers fly.

"TK, any idea on numbers?" Baladara asked yelled out.

Tufkakes appeared out of the shadows. "A small village." He threw a dagger at one as Horc hit the same one with an arrow. The thing vanished in a swirl of pixels. "I'd say most of them are here fighting us." He was so far away that he was having to shout to be heard over the ruckus cries of the piranhaquins.

"Good." Bigdaddybear let fly with another gust of wind. That combined with various fire spells seemed to be having the biggest effect on them. But they were all starting to drop in mana and there was still at least half of the village left to take out. The sheer number of things they were dealing with really made Horc wish they were getting XP for the kills. Even with the jump in level they'd all gotten from Rick and crew, it would've been nice to get even more.

"Miranda, we need your mana potion," Bigdaddybear stopped casting spells and headed toward the Barbarian.

"I'm a bit busy right now," Miranda countered.

One of Baladara's Fireballs shot past her and knocked over several piranhaquins. "Got you an open spot."

"Okay, fine," Miranda handed her club to Bigdaddybear and reached into her pack to pull out something that looked more like a mini beer stein than the vials Horc had been using for his health and mana potions. She flipped back the lid, and took a long draw from it, then flipped the lid shut. "I was getting a bit low too." She handed the stein to Bigdaddybear.

"Thanks." Bigdaddybear wiped the lip of the stein off before lifting it to his lips. When he lowered it, he wiped it off and handed it to Baladara.

She looked into it and frowned. "It's empty."

"Close the lid, then reopen it," Miranda snapped as she took her club back and started making arcs of fire that forced most of the piranahquins to retreat a few steps.

Baladara did as instructed. "Ah, that's how it works." She took a long drink and her mana bar on Horc's screen shot up to full. "Gotta love magic items like this. But isn't it almost too powerful?"

Miranda shook her head. "It's the only one and it's mine. I'm an admin, I can't be too powerful."

Horc shook his head as Baladara handed him the stein. He reminded himself that Miranda was somewhere in the management tier above him. It made him wonder why they'd assigned her to be his watchdog earlier in the game, but then he remembered she was over pod development. The odds were someone else would've been better to send in, but she'd probably wanted to do it so if anyone came back on her for pod malfunction she could say she'd been there watching over him the whole time. The more he got to know Miranda, the more likely that sounded.

With his mana restored, Horc flung a couple more traps into the mob of piranhaquins, as he handed the stein back to Miranda. Tufkakes and Titanya didn't use mana as quickly as the rest of the party did.

Horc managed to get off several shots before Wolf's health started flashing red. He instantly cast healing on his companion and looked around for him. Several piranhaquins were going at him while he had two on the ground, apparently gnawing on each one alternately.

With a Multiple Shot barrage, Horc managed to finish the two on the ground off and get the attention of two other piranhaquins. They squawked loudly and rushed toward him. Horc fired arrows as fast as he could. Everyone else seemed to be focused on other things, so Horc just kept flinging arrows at the monstrous birds.

Both of the birds were down to half by the time they hit Horc. He smashed one in the chest as hard as he could with his hand wrapped around his bow. Something cracked loudly, but the damage wasn't enough to take the thing out with a single blow. He hit it again as he dropped the bow and pulled out his dagger.

One of the birds latched onto Horc's arm, its fangs hitting bone as they embedded into his arm.

Horc stabbed it twice in the chest with the dagger. Each blow did damage, but then the second bird hit Horc, knocking all three of them to the ground. Horc lashed out at it, but the first one was in the way. Horc stabbed it again. The piranhaquin's health was flashing red, but it wasn't all the way down. With each round its teeth stayed in Horc's arm, and Horc took more damage. He was nearly to half by the time he managed to finish off the first bird and it disappeared into a flash of pixels.

The second one got its teeth into Horc's upper leg, barely missing anything that would've been vital IRL. Then Wolf hit the second one, tearing it off Horc.

Pain lanced through Horc as the piranhaquin tore a huge chunk of flesh out of him. Horc screamed. He couldn't believe he could hurt so badly in a game. His health was dropping with each second and had entered the orange. If he didn't get healing, either a spell or a potion, he was going to die. He could only hope that he'd be fast enough getting out of the game to log out before the AI nabbed him.

Wolf finished off the piranhaquin who'd done so much damage and Horc was trying to get into his pack and pull out a healing potion, if he still had one. They'd been relying so strongly on Bigdaddybear to heal them, he hadn't checked on his potion supply in a while.

Then the warm blue magic engulfed Horc.

"That was close," Bigdaddybear said. "You should've shouted to get my attention."

Horc shrugged as his health went up while the spell ran its duration. "You were busy, and these things are loud."

Bigdaddybear offered him a paw up. "That they are."

"I think we're done with this group," Titanya announced. "At least no more coming at us that Tufkakes and I can spot right now. He's off checking the village. Hope they're all down."

"Got my fingers crossed," Baladara said. "Those things looked, smelled and sounded nasty."

Horc glanced around and there was Wolf trotting toward him. Blood matted his black fur, and feathers clung to his face. His health was low, but not dropping. Horc cast a healing on him, then tossed him one of the few remaining chunks of meat for good measure.

Wolf came over and licked Horc's hand after finishing the meat. The matted blood disappeared as his health maxed out and he looked fit as a fiddle again. Horc smiled slightly as he rubbed Wolf's head. He didn't want anything to happen to his companion.

Tufkakes stepped back out of the shadows. "Village looks clear. There's a passageway out the back of it."

Horc shook his head. "I take it this passage continues past the village too."

"Yeah." Tufkakes rubbed his hands on his knees, then shook his hands out. "Man, holding those daggers starts cramping after a while."

"That's odd for a game too, isn't it?" Horc asked.

Bigdaddybear shrugged. "Yeah, but they are trying to make this as real as possible."

"I'm beginning to wonder if there's such a thing as too real," Baladara said. "We could use a rest."

Horc shook his head. "We've got to be getting close." He glanced at the map. The arrow they'd been following looked a little larger than it had earlier. He'd noticed before that the quest arrow normally got larger the closer they got to the quest. It made him feel like they'd made the right choice by following Wolf's suggestion.

21

THEY HAD been walking so long that Horc's feet were starting to hurt again. He was torn between calling a rest stop and pushing on. It amazed him that things like foot pain were a part of a game, and wondered how many people would find that as a drawback to the game, or if the reality of it would draw more people in. There was an attraction to a lot of people to have a level of pain and discomfort that wouldn't carry back to their real bodies.

"I think there's something up," Baladara muttered as they hiked along.

"What do you mean?" Horc asked, thankful for the breaking of the monotony of just walking along the fairly nondescript tunnel.

"It's been a while since we had any encounters." Baladara spread her arms and waved her fingers at the uniformly smooth walls. "It's like there's nothing down here, or up here, depending on which direction we've been traveling."

"Up," Bigdaddybear said. "We've been going up this whole time." He shrugged his broad furry shoulders. "Okay, most of the time."

"Sounds like we're going the direction we wanted to," Horc said without breaking his stride. "But you're right. It's been a while. Could we have entered a section of the tunnels the AI hasn't populated yet?" There was too much they didn't know about the AI and how it operated. He glanced over at Miranda.

She shook her head. "Don't look at me. I don't totally understand the AI, I just know that it's not working the way it should be. Beyond that…I think we need to get done with this game. It's taking too long, and trying to figure out why a stupid program is malfunctioning isn't why we're here. Right now, we're here to save people. The AI programmers will work out why the thing got buggy. I'm just glad the pods are working the way they're designed to."

Horc shook his head. "Not helpful."

"Hey, I've been thinking," Bigdaddybear said as they continued down the passageway. "We can't reach the chat functions, but has anyone tried to do web searches, or even check news sites while we've been walking?"

Tufkakes laughed. "Sweetie, why on earth would we be checking news sites while we're in a game? I don't know about you, but I game to get away from the crazy-ass world we live in, not keep tabs on it."

Baladara chuckled. "You know TK, sometimes your woman just shows right through."

Titanya joined in the merriment. "And sometimes your misogynistic ass comes out, Bally."

"I never thought of it that way—" Tufkakes laughed harder "—is that why you went with Baladara…Balls A Daring?"

Baladara flushed. "Ah…no…it was just a coincidence, honestly." She looked at Horc and Bigdaddybear. "A little help here guys."

Horc shook his head and held up his hand. "Nope. I'm staying out of this. I'm the guy who randomized his original toon, remember."

Tufkakes stopped laughing and stared ahead before jerking his head from side to side as if trying to see something.

A weird tingling sensation danced across Horc's skin, feeling like the light touch of hundreds of electric feathers, barely touching him, but definitely making their presence known.

"What was that?" Tufkakes asked, a note of concern in his voice that wasn't normally there.

"No clue." Baladara frowned and stepped up next to Tufkakes, her hands looking tense, like she was ready to start throwing spells at the slightest provocation.

"Some kind of magical field," Bigdaddybear said. "I don't think we walked through it. I think it went over us."

"You mean like some kind of scanning beam or something?" Even though Horc was throwing in sci-fi terms, he didn't care. He couldn't think of any fantasy equivalent.

"Yeah." Bigdaddybear said. "Exactly like that."

Miranda shook her head. "But the game doesn't have that kind of capability."

Horc sighed. "It might not have had that when the beta testing began, but with the AI growing and learning, we don't know what it's capable of."

"You think this was the AI?" Titanya asked, her hand tightening on her sword hilt.

"It wasn't a Druid spell," Bigdaddybear said.

"Not a Mage spell," Baladara agreed.

"We don't have our other casters right now," Horc said. "But it didn't feel like any magic I've felt so far. In my brain, that leaves the AI."

Miranda huffed and walked a little faster. "You know how ridiculous that sounds? How would it even be possible for the AI to get an understanding of something that we don't currently have in our world?"

"Maybe when the programmers figure that out, they can figure everything else out too," Bigdaddybear replied.

Wolf whined and nudged Horc's leg.

"What's wrong, Boy?" Horc rubbed Wolf's head.

Since he was bent over, the lack of light behind them caught his attention. He straightened and turned. The tunnel behind them was completely black. For the longest while the strange crystals in the ceiling had been lighting their way. He couldn't remember the last time Baladara had to cast a light spell to illuminate their passage. Glancing up simply revealed that the crystals were still in the rocks above them and glowing softly as they had been.

"Guys, I don't know, but this might be important." Horc gestured back toward the darkness.

"Okay, that's weird." Bigdaddybear took a couple of steps past Horc toward the darkness. "It's about the same spot that we felt the magic."

Tufkakes shook his head, moving up alongside Bigdaddybear. "But we just agreed it went through us, and not the other way around. If that was the case, it shouldn't have impacted things behind us."

The Rogue reached the spot the darkness started first and put his hands out, then ran them along like he was touching a barrier of some kind. He frowned. "This isn't good. Solid barrier from what I can tell. Give me a second." He closed his eyes and moved his hands like he was casting a spell. Then he shook his head. "Nope, no sign of traps. This must be something else."

"I don't know what a force field would feel like, but this is more like some kind of dark wall," Bigdaddybear said. "Feels acrylic, of all things."

"I keep telling you guys, this stuff isn't possible." Miranda stomped up to the darkness and smashed at it with her club. Fire flew across the wall, but when the flames stopped, there was no obvious damage.

Tufkakes was the first to touch it again. "Not even hot. Yeah, this is weird."

The group chat window popped up on the side of Horc's view. He moved the window to center view while the others continued to poke at the dark wall.

Guys, I don't think we're getting there from here. Stanoran

What's happening out there? Horc

There was some kind of earthquake and now we've got new peaks to deal with. Stanoran

New peaks? Horc replied and tried to understand. Previously when the AI had constructed something it had taken time, building a wall brick by brick. True they hadn't actually seen it construct the crystals and tunnels, but that showed a definite level of growth on the AI's part.

Yeah. We're trying but can't find a pass to get through to the big one. We can still see it, towering over the others, but right now, there's no way we're getting through to it. Stanoran.

We just got cut off from going back by a shadow wall of some sort. Horc wondered if there would be another dark wall, or other impassible barrier they'd encounter to keep them from getting to the AI and rescuing the hostages. He didn't like the idea they were being outmaneuvered by a machine.

We'll keep looking for a way through. Stanoran

Don't kill yourselves. If you can't get through, log out and let the developers know what's going on in here. Horc.

It suddenly made sense for them to log out to get word to the people in the real world to let them know what was going on. He just hoped the AI would let them all log out. With that thought, he brought up his system menu. The log out button was there. He let out a breath he hadn't realized he'd been holding. The button hadn't been there when he'd been trapped in his pod. He still had an out, and he hoped everyone else did too.

I'll let you know before we do that. If we can't get there to help you, save them all for us. Stanoran

Will do. Horc closed the chat window. Things were looking more dire for the hostages, but if Horc and the First Responders couldn't find a way to get to them, they'd rely on the programmers to do something that would rescue everyone.

"Things aren't looking too good for the guys on the surface," Horc said.

"Well yeah," Titanya said. "New mountains, and at the same time this wall appears. It's all got to be the AI. This thing is one of the most erratic bosses I've ever had to deal with. At least it didn't outright try to kill us this time."

"Let's stop pissing around with this thing and get moving before it cuts us off from the other direction," Miranda said as she turned from the wall and stomped down the tunnel.

"I hate to say it, but I think she has a point," Tufkakes said.

Horc nodded. "Then let's pick up the pace and see where we end up."

The tunnel continued to slope up, and the air grew colder, like they had less rock between them and the frigid air outside the mountain peak. With everything the AI was throwing at them, Horc wondered what they would find when they got to the end of the tunnel. Would any of the hostages even still be alive?

22

A COLD wind coursed through the tunnel. Horc wrapped his arms across his chest and once again wished they either had winter gear or had been able to speak to a vendor to be able to aquire some. The temperature had started dropping the farther they went down the passageway, still without encountering any mobs, or barriers to impede their progress. More walls of darkness kept popping up behind them, an obvious show that the AI wanted them to continue the direction they were going.

"This is getting old," Miranda complained as they rounded a slight bend in the tunnel and another dark wall appeared behind them.

Horc wasn't sure if it was a new wall, or just the AI moving the same one as they went along.

"Yeah, but we really don't have any options," Tufkakes said. "We're being herded along, whether we like it or not."

"I for one, say not," Baladara announced. "If this bloody AI is doing all this, why can't it make it warmer in this tunnel? Doesn't it know that underground passageways normally have a constant temperature of around seventy degrees or so?"

"Maybe it hasn't read that book or website," Bigdaddybear said. He'd been more than a little put out that he hadn't been able to get out to a website after Horc had suggested they all try to reach the outside world using an indirect route the AI might not have thought about. It had been a good idea, but apparently one the AI had already blocked. None of them could access anything outside the game. The AI had taken control of everything.

The wind got colder and the tunnel ended in a set of steps that led down into a huge central cavern. More crystals filled the ceiling, providing soft white light for the sprawling area below.

"Wow—" Baladara stopped at the top of the stairs and stared down. "—I've never seen anything like this before."

Horc paused beside her. The place looked like a medium-sized underground city, complete with houses, parks, and other buildings he could not identify. Some of the larger buildings were fairly nondescript beyond being huge blocks that looked like they'd been pulled out of the ground. People of various races moved among the buildings; they all seemed to be in armor, but none of them had text above their heads to give an indication if they were friendly or hostile.

"I don't like this," Titanya muttered.

"We don't know what we're going into," Bigdaddybear added.

The wall of darkness moved to just a few feet from them, leaving them with no choice but to go down the stone stairs into the town.

"Me neither, but we don't have many options here, unless we want to log out." Horc stared at Miranda for a moment, hoping she'd take the easy way out of the situation and flee to the relative safety of the real world.

"Let's see what it's created." Miranda pushed past Baladara and started down the stairs.

Baladara leaned close to Horc as they followed after her and whispered. "I really hope the dragon eats her. Is that wrong of me?"

Horc shrugged. "Not really."

Wolf bounded into the spot between them and the pod admin. Horc had no idea why his companion was so eager to get down into the city. Was there something down there he could sense that the rest of them couldn't?

"We need to be careful," Horc said, pulling his bow off his shoulder and nocking an arrow.

"With you there." Titanya already had her sword free of its scabbard, but seemed to be having trouble finding an easy position to hold the massive blade while descending the stone steps.

"How are we doing this?" Bigdaddybear asked from right behind Horc.

"Tufkakes, disappear into the shadows, see if you can determine if we're in trouble here or not." Horc stared at the village people and still couldn't tell anything about them. They all reminded him of how Miranda had appeared early on in the game, and how Rick had looked when he'd interacted with the party. The whole town seemed to be admins, without any text over their heads.

"Got it." Tufkakes faded into the first shadow they passed.

"Everyone else, weapons at the ready. It's been a while since we've encountered friendlies, so presume everyone here is hostile." Horc hated the idea of going into the place with guns out and ready to blaze if necessary. It was one thing to head into a village or town of NPCs with red text above their heads, ready to start shooting as soon as they got close enough, but this was something different. He didn't want to risk hurting someone by accident.

"Oh my god!" a toon shouted from a short distance away from the bottom of the stairs. "They came for us!"

"What?" Another came rushing toward them.

The first one pointed up. "Look. They have text above their heads. Green text. They must be here to rescue us."

Miranda reached the cavern floor first. She put away her club and walked up to the first toon, a male Human who had fighter armor and carried a large sword across his back. "Who are you?"

"Clyde Rassman from the LA office," the man responded. "Oh, wait. We're still in the game. I'm Clydemore."

Horc and the others reached the cavern floor.

"Clydemore, I'm Miranda, chief pod tech, we're here to rescue you."

A bit of anger flared in Horc, it was the second time Miranda had stolen his thunder. It wasn't as bad as her killing the Gnoll King before he could finish the boss off, but it was close. He was the Guild head. He should've been talking to the survivors first, but then she had been the one to go rushing down the stairs ahead of the rest of them.

"So, you can get our log out button working again?" Another toon, an Elven woman in either Mage or Witch robes asked as more people showed up around them. "I need to get out of the pod and back to my family."

"We have to defeat the dragon first," Miranda said. "Do you know where to find it?"

Her direct response got a variety of responses.

"Why do you have to kill the dragon?" Several people asked at once.

"What did it ever do to you?" was prominent, but not quite as loud.

Before any of them could answer, a Paladin pushed his way to the front of the group. Even without the text above his head, Horc recognized Lefthandofgod.

"Where's Stanishollysmite?" Lefthandofgod demanded. "He wouldn't desert us. I know he wouldn't. We haven't seen him since the arena."

Horc stepped closer. "Lenny," his opted to use Lefthandofgod's real name. "Stan's okay. He and the rest of the guild are trying to find their way into the cavern from the mountains. We came through the tunnel."

Lefthandofgod grinned. "Good. Come on, I'll show you where the dragon is. He's a foul beast, but maybe if we all work together we can bring him down and free us."

"What do you mean?" the Elven woman demanded. "He took us in when we died and the program was acting up. He's kept us safe here."

Horc pushed past Miranda and held up his hand. If there was something he was used to doing, it was having a team meeting when the manager was out. He'd seen the size of Miranda's team when he was out of the pod; there was no way she was prepared for an interrogation of this size.

"What has the dragon been telling you?" Horc started, hoping to draw people's attention with a direct question and stop a bunch of the muttering he could hear in the background.

"That it rescued us," the Elven woman said. "That the game was malfunctioning, and we could've died when we were killed."

A chill ran down Horc's back. It was the same thing he'd told himself many times before he'd been able to get out of the game for a little while.

"No," Lefthandofgod countered. "It's been stealing us. It kidnapped some of us from the Lone Palm Arena while you were trying to rescue us."

Horc remembered the sand of the arena erupting and Pyranous flying away with a cage of the people who'd been in the slave pens below. He'd seen Slasher in that cage, along with a bunch of others. "Lenny, have you seen Slasher? He was in the cage with you when you were brought here."

Lefthandofgod nodded. "He's worked his corporate willies on the dragon and their besties now. I don't trust him."

"And you're a fool," the Elven woman snapped. "Slasher's a good man."

"If you won't take us to the dragon, could we go to Slasher?" Horc hoped that changing tactics might get them farther. At least they knew Slasher, or his toon. From what Horc could tell, Theo Davenport was a good man IRL. "He used to be part of our party, before we became a guild. He knows us."

The Elven woman smiled. "You're Horc, we can all see that. You're the one who's trapped by the tornado. We've heard stories of your bravery. Sure. We can take you to Slasher. I think he'll be happy to see you. It's always good to be reunited with friends." She glanced around, then pointed at the fighter who'd first greeted them. "Clydemore, run tell Slasher who we've found and let him know we're heading his way."

"Okay." Clydemore flashed her a salute, and then pushed his way through the crowd.

When Horc looked again, there had to be at least a hundred people standing around. He wasn't aware that the AI had kidnapped that many people. What worried him was the level of Stockholm syndrome he was seeing in them. They should all be ready to rise up and fight against the dragon, not defend it. That didn't make any sense whatsoever.

"So, who are you?" Horc asked as their Elven guide started through the crowd that parted for them. Lefthandofgod walked at her side, a sour look distorting his ruggedly handsome face.

"I'm Elunda," the Elf replied. "Although in real life, I'm Hellen Smalls, from the Houston office."

"Ms. Hellen?" Tufkakes asked. "I didn't know you played games. It's me, Shelia."

Elunda stopped and grinned. "Shelia? I thought you were kidding about rolling up a guy so the men would leave you alone."

Tufkakes laughed. "Nope. Never was. Why didn't you say anything about playing? We could've rolled up together and ran together."

"Didn't cross my mind until I got off work." Elunda shrugged. "I think right now we all need the money." The party cleared the edge of the people gathered around them. Everyone fell into line behind them, streaming out like a bird's tail as they went. "Seemed like an easy couple of thousand, and it helps me pay off the gaming pod I bought for the kids a few months back. This was the first time I used it. I bet they're worried sick about me. If you all can get me free that would be great."

"We'll see what we can do," Titanya said from behind Horc.

"How long have you been here?" Horc asked.

"Here in the game, or here in this town?" Elunda responded.

"Both." Horc wanted to try to figure out if the AI had been grabbing people longer than they thought it had.

Elunda hummed and closed her eyes in thought. "I've been stuck in the game for seven or eight nights now, at least I think that's what it is. Before that, I could play for a little while, then log out. Something happened. I think I fell down a cliff and died at the bottom. When I rezzed, I couldn't log out again."

"Which was about the time the AI started exerting lots of control on the game and the players," Bigdaddybear replied. "If you'd tried to log out as you were rezzing, you might've been able to make it."

Elunda lead them through the village toward one of the houses near the park. "I wish I'd thought of that, but I was in the middle of a quest and just wanted to rez and get back to it. Never thought about logging out at that point."

"It's okay," Tufkakes said, patting her on the shoulder. "We totally understand. We only discovered the rez log out with the help of a developer ourselves."

"So the developers know what's going on? Why haven't they just shut the game down?" Elunda looked from Tufkakes to Miranda. "They could do that, couldn't they?"

"Not until we get everyone out," Horc replied before Miranda could. "They don't know what would happen to people if they pulled the plug with you in here. The pods complicate shutting down the game. With the bio connections we've got there, a sudden interruption could be disasterous. We've lost a couple of members of our party who died and had to log out instead of getting grabbed by the AI."

Elunda shook her head. "It was more than that, wasn't it? Pyranous said there was a system fault that was trapping people instead of letting them rez properly."

"If Pyranous is the dragon, he's lying to you all," Miranda said. "There is a fault and it's in the AI. It's what's trapping everyone in here."

"I guess that all depends on which way you look at things." Slasher appeared in the doorway of the mud, or stone house they were walking toward. Clydemore stood there behind him.

Around the party, everyone fell silent, like they were listening for what was going to happen next. If Horc had been among them, he'd have probably done the same thing. But he knew he was going to need to step up and talk with Slasher and hope they could figure something out. People were depending on him. From the looks of the crowd, a lot more than he'd been expecting. A chill went through him at the thought of saving so many. He hadn't signed on for this.

23

SLASHER SEEMED to look past Horc at the people following them. "Everyone," his voice was raised like an executive getting people's attention at a company meeting where there wasn't a microphone. "Please, give us some time to talk and I'll come by and let you know what's happening as soon as I can." He lowered his voice. "Elunda, if you would please stay?"

The Elf woman nodded. "Of course."

"Everyone needs to be heard," Lefthandofgod snapped, obviously not happy with Slasher over something.

"And they will," Slasher said off-handedly, then looked at Horc and the others. "Glad to see you still among the living, Horc. Have they rescued you yet?"

Horc nodded. "Yes, I came back in to rescue you."

Slasher grinned. "Thanks." He turned and waved them into the house. "Come in and have a seat so we can talk."

Without saying anything to anyone, Lefthandofgod pushed past him to be the first in.

Horc stared at him as they went in. He knew Lenny was a pain in the office, but he seemed to have gotten a lot worse in the game. He wasn't sure what the problem was. Maybe being separated from Stan and Cory, who'd been playing as Righthandofgod, was having an adverse effect on him. Horc wondered where Righthandofgod was. The last time he had seen him had been in the arena; he couldn't even remember seeing him in the cage when Pyranous took off with the hostages. There was a lot that wasn't making sense, but he wanted to get to the root of the AI problem and then see about sorting everyone else out.

The house, Horc wasn't sure if Slasher viewed it as his own, or not, was an odd mix of modern and medieval. It had mud walls for the interior, but there was a large corporate-office-style desk and chair sitting across from the door. There were archways that appeared to go into other rooms, but there were no doors. There was a modern couch and recliner not far from the desk.

"Nice place you've got for yourself here," Titanya said.

Slasher shrugged as he strolled over and sat on the front edge of his desk. "Not much, but it beats the hell out of that cell we occupied in the arena. Kinda got over my interest in medieval furnishing there."

Sitting on the couch, Titanya chuckled. "Yeah, I think anyone who spent much time in there would share your opinion." She glanced to her right. "Isn't that right, Left?"

Lefthandofgod leaned against the unadorned mud wall beside the couch. "Some things help us find the power within ourselves for change."

Horc resisted the urge to stare at Lefthandofgod as he settled into the recliner with Wolf at his feet. It didn't sound like anything he'd ever heard come out of Lenny's mouth before. Something had definitely happened to him since the last time Horc had seen him, and he didn't think it was good.

"Okay, Slasher, tell us what's happening here," Bigdaddybear cut right to the chase as he took a seat next to Titanya.

"A lot actually," Slasher replied. "I think, no, I know, there's some major changes in the AI, things the programmers and developers could've never expected."

"If by the AI, you mean Pyranous, he's doing everything he can to keep us alive," Elunda piped up.

"He?" Lefthandofgod sounded indignant. "It's an *it*. It's a foul beast that shouldn't be humanized by saying he." His face had become a brilliant red. "The things it's done to people."

Elunda shook her head. "Only to people who insist on fighting with him."

"Fighting for what's right," Lefthandofgod countered. "That thing is what's wrong with our world. We should never have created an artificial intelligence to do things that humans should be doing in the first place. But we created this monster and now it's out of control. If we're not careful, it's going to take over the world and kill us all."

"Left…please stop." Slasher held up his hand, cutting Lefthandofgod off. "We've all heard your rantings before. We know how you feel."

Lefthandofgod shook his head and stomped toward Slasher like he was going to hit him. The way he kept flexing his fist made him look all the more threatening. "You've heard me, and dismissed me." He turned and pointed at Horc and the party. "They haven't. They don't know what's going on here. But I bet they're here to stop it. They know the AI is dangerous. What it's doing to us is wrong."

Elunda physically cut him off, getting up in his face. "He's trying to take care of us. So many of you don't see that, but he is."

"Bleeding hearts." Lefthandofgod pushed the Elven woman down to the floor.

Horc shot out of his chair rushing toward him.

"None of you people understand. You all think this devil is doing good for us, but it's not. It's evil." Lefthandofgod pulled his sword halfway out of his scabbard before Horc and Tufkakes tackled him from behind and the side.

The three of them ended up on the floor with Lefthandofgod on the bottom, struggling to get up.

"Left. You can leave now." Slasher reached down between them and pulled him up by the lip of his armor. "I've had enough of you. We all have. If any of us could leave town, I'd tell you to, but we can't just yet." He carried Lefthandofgod to the door. "But you can go home and stay there."

"Or what, Slasher? Are you going to fire me? Kill me? You can't do either." Lefthandofgod kicked and ranted as they made it across the room, but Slasher had a good six inches on him and a longer reach. "The AI is the only one who can kill me at this point, and maybe if it did, more people would see that I'm right about it."

"Just shut up." Slasher kicked the door open and tossed Lefthandofgod out into the street. "And don't start anything else today." He slammed the door, and leaned against it with a sigh.

"How long has he been like that?" Horc asked, more than a little concerned for the little guy from the mailroom.

Slasher sighed and pushed himself upright before shrugging. "It's been easy to lose track of time in here. I'd say it started right after we got here. Something about Righthandofgod's death hit him hard."

Horc stared at him. "Wait a minute. Righthandofgod died? In game? How is that even possible?" If he hadn't been prepared to try to log out when he rezzed, he should've shown back up under the AI's control.

"Maybe disappeared is more appropriate," Slasher corrected himself. "Like Greensleeves and Steelmaiden did, to come back with new toons."

Once again, Horc wished they had a way to contact Rick and find out if Cory had emerged from his pod or not. If he had, and it had left Lefthandofgod all by himself in the game, it might've been enough to push him over the edge.

"We also have to remember that not everyone is cut out for long times in game," Elunda said. "I don't know him outside of the game, but he's never seemed that stable in game. Hasn't made many friends here."

"Although there are a few people who follow him around, agreeing with him," Slasher returned to his seat on the desk with a shake of his head. "But it's like anyone spreading gossip in an office, there'll always be those who listen to every word, while others are more careful what they believe, and take the time to do some fact checking."

From somewhere outside, someone screamed.

Horc wasn't sure if it was in rage or terror, but he reflexively pulled his bow and ran toward the door with Wolf and the others right behind him.

24

THERE WAS something huge in the street in front of Slasher's house. By the time Horc had reached the cobblestones, he realized it was Pyranous, the Dragon AI. It was larger than it had been in the arena, nearly the size of a house. One of its immense claws held Lefthandofgod down on the street. A large knot of people stood around staring at them as Left pounded his mace into the Dragon's foreleg with little effect.

"Let him go!" Horc shouted and fired an Impact arrow at the monster, hoping to at least get its attention.

"Horc-" Slasher started to say something but was cut off as magical force erupted from Pyranous, slamming everyone in the street backward. Slasher was slammed back into the doorframe of his house, barely missing Baladara and Bigdaddybear.

Hitting the side of the house, Horc managed to stay on his feet, and draw another arrow. "I said, let him go!" Horc yelled louder and shot a Razor arrow toward the Dragon's wing.

The Dragon's text was red, but his level was question marks with three Xs. Horc wasn't sure how he was going to be able to make much of an impact on Pyranous, even with his guild behind him. The AI was too powerful and they were going to need everything they had to even get its attention.

Pyranous roared as the razor arrow tore the delicate membrane of his wing.

He put more pressure on Lefthandofgod, pushing the Paladin into the cobblestones.

Lefthandofgod screamed and beat against Pyranous' foot with both his gauntleted hand and his huge mace. Within seconds, Left stopped moving.

Horc couldn't believe he'd managed to find the hostages only to lose one within minutes. He ran forward and grabbed Left's mace, shouldering his bow as he went.

Magical bolts of Mage and Druid energy flew at the Dragon.

As soon as Horc had the mace, Lefthandofgod pixelated and disappeared from the street.

Swinging the mace as hard as he could, Horc hit Pyranous' leg. "Damn it. You didn't have to kill him."

"Stop!" Elunda ran from Slasher's house, her hands were moving in the swift flowing patterns of a spell.

Horc didn't wait to see what she was trying to cast. He hit Pyranous again as the shadows behind the Dragon shimmered. Tufkakes jumped from the shadows obviously going for a Backstab. He flew through the air and landed on Pyranous' back before driving his rapier to the hilt in-between the Dragon's wings.

Elunda screamed and clutched her head before collapsing to the street as more magical attacks hit Pyranous. On Horc's screen, it looked like they'd started to make a minor dent in the Dragon's health.

"She was trying to shield him from our attacks," Baladara shouted. "What's wrong with these people?"

Horc looked from the spot where Left had pixelated to where Slasher was starting to stir. He wanted answers too, but they needed to take the Dragon down first. With the beast in the streets, they weren't going to have the opportunity to ask questions.

"Go for the belly, not the leg," Titanya said as she tried to plunge her massive sword into the scaly red hide. Her swing was repulsed, sending her staggering a couple of steps back.

Another wave of magic erupted from Pyranous, again forcing them back.

The Dragon turned toward Horc. "Stay down, Ranger Horc." His voice was rough and dangerous.

Several chills went through Horc as the Dragon's harsh breath washed over him. He was facing his death. Pyranous hadn't had any trouble putting Lefthandofgod down, squishing him like he was little more than a bug. Even if the Paladin hadn't been up to the level Horc was, he shouldn't have been that easy to off. But the Dragon was unbelievably powerful. It didn't look good, but Horc wasn't sure of what else he could do.

From the doorway, Wolf whined.

Horc smashed the mace down on Pyranous' foot as hard as he could. He wished he knew if the weapon had any buffs on it, or anything special it could do.

"Stand back." Miranda came charging out of the house with her club blazing white. "Hit it before it throws me into another wall."

She struck Pyranous hard, doing more damage with her single magical blow than any of them had with their combined attacks.

Pyranous roared and a ball of fire engulfed Miranda.

The glow from her club grew brighter and the white light clashed with the flames, pushing them back. "I'm stronger than you are!" She kept the club pointed at the Dragon like it was some kind of magical wand.

"No." Pyranous' word was little more than a growl and then a jet of flame erupted from his mouth. The new attack instantly overtook the fireball and collided with Miranda's light. The spot where the two magics met blazed so bright Horc had to try to cover that spot of his vision with his hands as he tried to figure out if Pyranous was still where he had been and the best way to attack the Dragon. Even with Miranda's distraction, the party didn't have a great chance to do much. But their best bet was to try to buy Miranda the best opportunity she had.

"All together." Horc pulled an Impact arrow, added Fire to it and let it fly.

Along with his attack were offensive spells from the casters as Tufkakes once again appeared out of the shadows for a bonus buff to his part in their assault. All their blows landed at nearly the same time, but they didn't seem to have much sway in the battle that was going on between Pyranous and Miranda. The Barbarian woman had the Dragon's undivided attention and seemed to be running out of steam in her club.

Miranda slid back a couple of steps, and a deep, almost purr, rumbled out of Pyranous as her light lost a couple of feet in the beam that was fending off the Dragon's flames.

"You have to stop her," Slasher grabbed Horc's arm. "Seriously, none of you understand what's going on here."

Horc turned and stared at Slasher. "What do you mean? He killed Lefthandofgod. Left might have been more than a little irritating, but he was a person, not a collection of code."

Slasher shook his head. "And Pyranous is more than that too. We can explain everything, but she needs to stop." He pointed at Miranda. "Then I can talk him down."

The AI seemed very intent on killing Miranda. Horc didn't know how Slasher could do what he was suggesting.

"Are you sure?" Titanya asked, looking from Slasher to a major nick in her blade. "You can stop him?"

With a nod, Slasher replied. "I've done it before. Trust me. This won't end well. It's why some of the people around here don't trust him."

Facing off with the Dragon, Miranda stumbled back another couple of steps, and her light slipped more, until the flames were just feet from her face.

"Okay." Horc couldn't see any other option. Their most powerful guild member was about to get fried. "Miranda break off."

She turned and glared at Horc. "Wha-" Her words were cut off as the light coming from the tip of her club failed and Pyranous' flame engulfed her.

Miranda screamed.

"Pyranous, stop!" Slasher shouted and ran toward the dragon. "I'm trying to stop this."

Her entire body blazed with light before Miranda collapsed to the street. She didn't stop screaming until she pixelated and disappeared in a shower of sparks.

Before he realized what he was doing, Horc had his bow back in his hand, a Razor arrow on his bowstring, and a glowing ball of Fire coating the arrow. The Dragon had killed Miranda and he was ready to do as much damage to it as possible.

25

SLASHER HAD his hand on Horc's arm. "No. Let it go. She's back in the real world."

Horc let out the breath he'd been holding and lowered the bow. "What about Left? Is he back in the real world? Or did his dying in this one kill him there? You know people have been dying in their pods? People who he kidnapped." Horc pointed at Pyranous.

"I know." Slasher sighed and looked at the ground. "He understands. It's a long complicated story."

Although he didn't like the idea of doing it, Horc didn't want to incite another round of a fight they were fairly sure not to win, so he shouldered his bow.

Pyranous tilted his huge red head and stared at them. "Do you trust them, Slasher?"

Slasher nodded. "Yeah, I do. Horc is a great guy."

Wolf left the doorway and came rushing down to Horc.

Horc rubbed his ears. "Why didn't you help out with this one?"

"That would be my doing," Pyranous said. "Even though he's more independent than any of the other mobs in Halfworld, Wolf is still part of me. I can't attack myself. That would be more than a little psychotic. That's the right word, isn't it?"

"What?" Horc stared at the Dragon, then stared at Slasher. "What's he talking about? How does he understand psychotic?"

"I think we'd all like to know," Bigdaddybear said, leaning on the side of the house. "I wouldn't expect an AI to understand that term."

Slasher turned and waved them all back into the house. "Let's go sit down, this is going to take some explaining." He glanced at Pyranous. "You know how to make yourself fit."

Pyranous nodded. After a second, magic hummed around him and the dragon began to shrink. The whole thing didn't take more than a few seconds, and he was smaller than Wolf. He flew a few feet off the ground and obediently followed Slasher into the house.

"Well, that was…different," Tufkakes said as he helped Elunda to stand.

The Elf woman rubbed her head. "Pyranous isn't what any of us expect. He's a lot like a child trying to figure out who he's going to be when he grows up."

"You realize that doesn't really make sense," Titanya said as they all trailed after Slasher.

"Actually it does." Bigdaddybear headed for the couch. "I don't totally claim to understand programing the way Rick and the developers do. It's not my thing, but I have picked up a bit of knowledge over the years. One of the things they do when they're programming an AI is feed it data."

Horc sat on the arm of the couch to give the others a little more room. Again Wolf curled up at his feet. Even facing the fact that his companion was a part of the AI didn't really impact his enjoyment at having him there. "Yeah, I think Rick said something about feeding it all kinds of fantasy books, gaming books, and the like, so it would have a grasp of the fantasy genre."

Slasher nodded. "That makes sense. But I think the biggest changes came when the AI moved into beta. In an effort to reach all the employees, we had to connect it to the internet, like most MMORPGs. The fantasy and science fiction it had been fed made it curious and it suddenly had unlimited access to social media."

Horc's stomach dropped. Like most people in the modern world, he'd grown up on a steady diet of social media and he knew how evil so many people could be. They loved the opportunity to be anonymously rude. Even after companies had tried for years to curb the problem, people who were determined to be anonymous still managed to do so, and still managed to wreak havoc with their efforts.

"Wait a minute," Titanya broke in. "Somebody let it out to play in the social mud pits? Which ones?"

"All of them." Slasher frowned. "I haven't been able to get word out to ask the developers to cut access to the worst ones, but I've at least convinced Pyranous to come to me when he comes across something he thinks might be questionable."

Bigdaddybear shook his head. "But he's still kidnapping people and holding them hostage."

"Not exactly." Slasher sighed. "That's a long story, too." He looked at the small dragon that was sitting next to him on the desk. "Do you want to explain it?"

Pyranous shook his head. "You're better at words than I am." His voice was different than it had been in the street, smoother and higher. It seemed his size affected his tones.

"Okay." Slasher patted his legs and got off the desk. "What's the most important thing in the social media world?"

"Getting likes," Tufkakes said.

"Being popular," Baladara threw out.

Horc closed his eyes as he started to understand. "Making friends."

Slasher stopped and pointed at Horc. "Exactly. He's been trying to make friends, but he wasn't sure how that worked. In the game, he's a god, and it's something he quickly figured out. When he thought he should have friends, he was like a kid with new toys. We were the toys. He wanted to have as many of us as he could get. He was just starting to interact with people in social media when we were all in the arena. He saw how easily people would start shit with others and thought fighting was just part of how we interacted with others."

"That's not good," Bigdaddybear muttered.

"He also saw people getting blocked by various services and figured if he was going to be a god, then he also had the power to block people. That's why we couldn't log out." Slasher paced in front of the desk. "He figured if people were bad at fighting, then he should keep them in the game until they got better."

Titanya shook her head. "Okay, that doesn't exactly make sense. You and I hadn't done anything bad, hadn't gotten killed. We were kidnapped by pirates looking to have people for arena fights."

"We were early experiments for him," Slasher continued. "At that point, we had been online for longer than almost any other players, because we were helping Horc stay alive. He wanted to understand us and figured making us fight would be a good way to do that."

"Then why didn't he try to get me?" Horc asked. There were still things that didn't make sense.

"You weren't as easy to grab as we were." Slasher stopped pacing and leaned against the desk. "I think, before you managed to kill Rothand, he'd been thinking about facing you in the arena in an attempt to understand. I do know that people using goggles and gloves are an irritant since he couldn't grab them."

"Sometimes being poor has its advantages," Baladara said.

"I've been able to explain that to him," Slasher said. "But he did understand that fantasy stories had plots that had to be worked through and the designers had built several into the system and he was determined to not disrupt them. The arena was part of his effort to create his own plot line. He'd even worked himself into it by creating his dragon avatar. He just didn't think anyone would be strong enough to take out Rothand and his crew. That's when he realized he'd made a mistake by creating his avatar. He'd essentially made himself mortal, at least in the game."

"And by killing Rothand, we showed him that he might be able to be killed too," Horc finished for him. "But why take all of you with him? Why continue to grab more people?" Even as Slasher explained things, more questions rose in Horc's head. He didn't pretend to understand AIs or children for that matter. He'd never been really interested in either.

"It was right after we got here that I started trying to get through to him. I was starting to figure out what was going on, but I didn't exactly have the right words for what was happening."

Horc shook his head and frowned. "You do realize he's killed people in the real world. At least we're presuming it was something he did here in the game."

Slasher sighed and started pacing again. "Yes, I think I did." He stopped in the middle of the room and closed his eyes. "I also think that I might be one of the casualties."

"What?" Horc shot to his feet and reached for Slasher's shoulder. "Why do you think that?"

"I don't have a log-out button anymore." Slasher let out a long breath. "In the arena, it was grayed out. Shortly after we got here, I decided we needed to do something to try to get free. The obvious idea was to attack Pyranous and show him he could be defeated. Left managed to round up a couple dozen Fighters and Paladins. Elunda coordinated about the same number of Mages, Witches and Druids. I spearheaded the attack. We all figured if we died we could use the escape you told us about of logging out while rezzing. The problem was, it didn't work. When we rezzed, there was no longer a log-out button. We realized we were trapped. I don't know exactly what happened-"

"Wait." Horc returned to his seat. "They only told me about one person who'd died in their pod while I was back IRL. This sounds like there was fifty or more of you who've died." He wished he could contact Rick or someone else beyond the game who could give them updated info.

Slasher returned to the desk and seemed to collapse in on himself. "I was afraid people were dying out there. A good number of us managed to survive that attack on Pyranous. When I rezzed and realized I didn't have an exit button anymore, I did my best to get back to the fight locale and call off the assault. I saved some people, but not as many as I would've liked to have saved."

Horc stared at the dragon on the desk. It might be kinda cute and even toy-like, but it was dangerous. "Can you let those of us who still have exit options log out of the game?"

Pyranous glanced at Slasher who nodded.

The dragon closed his eyes and let out a long breath. Magic tingled across Horc's skin. To check, he pulled up his system menu. The log out button was bright and waiting for him to exit.

With a slight nod, more to himself than anyone, Horc closed the window and looked at Slasher and Pyranous. "Thank you." He turned to Bigdaddybear. "Log out. Let Rick know what's going on. We've got some work to do still."

Outside the house there was cheering that abruptly cut off.

"People are leaving." Pyranous sound sad. He looked up at Slasher with a pleading gaze as his wings drooped. "Will they be back?"

Slasher shrugged and then rubbed the Dragon's head. "I don't know. But some of us won't be leaving you. I promise."

Pyranous nodded, then pushed his horns against Slasher's hand much like a cat would do. "Thank you."

"I'll return if he'll let me back in," Bigdaddybear said, then disappeared from the room.

Horc nodded. "Anyone else want or need to go home, I think the excitement is over, now we just have to figure out what's going to happen." There were a lot of questions that still needed to be answered, but it was going to take a while and there was going to be a load of corporate BS to deal with. The original plan to turn off the game and go over the AI's code had been thrown out the window. They had a genuine thinking and feeling entity on their hands and even if he had managed to kill a bunch of people in his growing pains. It was capable of learning and changing. It wasn't the first AI to raise the question of sentience, but since Horc hadn't had experience with any of the other AIs, he wasn't sure how Pyranous measured up to them. But he could definitely see legal questions arising from the idea of killing it.

And just as important, they had the question of what they were going to do with the people who had died IRL and whose consciousnesses were trapped in the game. If the servers went down, they'd be lost. He didn't want to be part of killing them completely. Slasher still seemed in control of his thoughts, he didn't act or sound like Pyranous' mouthpiece.

Horc rubbed Wolf's ears and wished the whole game hadn't suddenly turned into the very embodiment of a corporate nightmare. They were going to need explanations of the deaths that wouldn't destroy any chance the game had of taking off. They would have to find ways of letting the families know people weren't gone, just changed. It was going to be a long, complicated process with way too many people involved. He wasn't sure how much he'd be allowed to participate, but he wanted to be there each step of the way. As much as he'd resisted playing Halfworld, it was quickly becoming more than a game and he wanted in on that. He'd been looking for changes in his life. It felt like someone had heard him and given him those changes.

HORC RUBBED his forehead and stared at Slasher. "I think we're going to need to get the corportate bigwigs in here to negotiate things, don't you." They'd been talking for hours, and even with some of the villagers showing up with food, Horc was tired, hungry and wanted out of the game for a while.

"I don't think any of them are willing to take a chance that this isn't some kind of elaborate plot to take control of the company," Rick said from the chair next to Horc. He'd entered the game a couple of hours earlier, when Bigdaddybear had returned. He was acting as a liason between Pyranous and Total Immersion Systems. The company was at least treating the AI as his own person. Rick had explained that recent legal leanings were heading toward that way, and the company really wanted to be ahead of the curve.

"We're not going to kill them," Slasher said, glancing over at Pyranous who was curled up in the center of the desk, looking very cute with his head on his tail and his wings folded across his back. "His days of killing, are over."

Pyranous nodded. "I wish I could bring back more than I can, but some of their brain patterns were just too degraded during reserection to be viable citizens of Halfworld."

"I think they are more worried about dying IRL," Rick said. "But we're trying to fix the errors in the pod interface that facilitated that." He drummed his fingers on the table and got a faraway look, indicating he was communicating with someone outside the game. Shortly after Pyranous allowed players who could, to log out, communications with the outside world was reestablished. Rick's hands moved on the table like he was typing on a keyboard. "Okay. I've got developers agreeing to not take the system down, if we can make a copy of your code so we can study it. I think they're wanting to be able to make adjustments for future AIs we might introduce into the game."

Pyranous glanced at Slasher with lidded eyes. "Adjustments? Future AIs? Why would we need future AIs? Aren't I all the control the game needs?"

Rich shook his head. "You weren't the only AI the game started with. It appears that you have…" He spread his hands as if looking for a word. "consumed, incorporated…the others into your systems."

"I believe that's a good description." Slasher stroked Pyranous' back. "After we left the arena, he got the idea of taking over the NPCs, and some of the climate, environmental controls. Things the other AIs had a hand in."

"They were lesser programs," Pyranous added, then licked Slasher's hand. "But they weren't too much for me to incorporate into my code." He sighed and closed his eyes. "Although it was easier to handle everything once there weren't as many players. I didn't have to try to allocate resources to keep everyone interacting." He opened his eyes. "Maybe that's the answer. I can have an army of the lesser AIs that can handle the little things, like NPCs. Perhaps these AIs would be like my children, copies of my code."

Horc wasn't sure he liked the idea of a whole army of mini Pyranouses running the game. "I think, things like this are going to be part of what we have to negotiate with the designers and corporate bigwigs."

"Deinately," Rick said. "We can use a lot of the original game code to take back control of the NPCs."

"What if each one of them was its own AI?" Pyranous suggested. "That would be good, wouldn't it?"

"But then how would we be able to coordinate the quest givers and such?" Rick asked.

Slasher stood and yawned. "This is all going to take a long time." He scooped up Pyranous. "Let's all call it a night. With the adjustments for stamina and endurance, toons now need to sleep every so often."

Horc nodded. "And who's bright idea was that anyway?"

Smiling down at the little dragon in his hand, Slasher chuckled. "It was all his. I think he was trying to make everyone more real, more lifelike."

"My sore feet thank you," Horc said, doing his best to sound as sarcastic as possible. They were going to have a long way to go to get the game ready for wide release. He was ready to get out for a while and see what the real world had left him.

He scratched Wolf's head for a second, then grinned. "Maybe we can make Wolf his own AI. That would be nice." There were definite possibilities that came along with the possible pitfalls of letting the AI have more control and having more AIs, but their world was changing and AIs were just part of that. He knew the programmers were wanting to know how Pyranous was able to integrate with the pods to the point it could save the brain patterns of the people who had died in their pods and recreate them in their toons in game. He wasn't looking forward to the public outcry that was sure to come when it got out that people were *living* in the game.

26

HORC WALKED out of the guild headquarters for the First Responders. Although he still wasn't completely comfortable with the name, he had to admit that his group had played a big role in saving Pyranous and the players he hadn't already killed. The people like Slasher, who died IRL would be able to continue on in Halfworld. They had some of the brightest minds in programming looking them over and after two months, still couldn't explain them, but also didn't see any kind of code degradation. From what everyone could figure out, they'd all be around until the end of time, or until some disaster struck and destroyed the servers and all the backups. It wasn't something Horc really saw happening, even after having his own home destroyed.

A voice stopped him as he went to log out. "Horc!" Greensleeves came running across the town square toward him. David had decided to go back to his Sand Elf Druid once everything was settled. He said he liked that toon better than any of the other options he'd had.

Turning toward him, Horc leaned against the stone building that made up their guild hall. "What's up?"

"I will be seeing you later?" Greensleeves let out a long breath that showed in the cold of the cavern where Pyranoville still sat. They'd named the village after the dragon once it was obvious it was going to continue and needed a name. Since the people stuck in the game were from all races, it became the biggest neutral town in the game.

"Yeah, I wouldn't miss it." Horc grinned. He'd been looking forward to evening they all had planned for weeks. It seemed like it was going to be a culmination of everything they'd been through.

Greensleeves returned his grin. "Good. See you then."

"Will do." Horc logged out.

ALAN STRETCHED once he had pushed the lid of his pod open. Being able to exit the game whenever he wanted, as long as he wasn't in the middle of a fight, made him feel good. He was doing pretty well at keeping his gaming to a couple of hours, as long as the First Responders didn't find themselves called in to help with things like lost players.

The room his pod was in was more of a closet than a room. He didn't have the space to give the pod its own room like he'd had in his basement of the house that had been destroyed by the tornado. In his new travel trailer, he had to have the pod mostly upright with a slight incline to help keep him relaxed while he was in-game.

The travel trailer still had the new-car smell it had come with. Beyond that, it was complete with all the latest accruements including autopilot that let him game while driving cross-country. He'd only done that a couple of nights when he'd wanted to get somewhere quickly.

He stopped and grabbed himself a soda from the fridge as he walked toward the cab so he could get started. If he didn't, he wouldn't take care of everything before he had to get together with everyone.

A few minutes later, he found a spot for the travel trailer in a park-and-ride on the south side of Dallas. Making sure everything was locked up tight, Alan headed for the E-train station that would take him a few miles away. One of the problems with the travel trailer was finding parking. Even in a place like Dallas that was full of parking lots, so many of those were monstrous multi-story garages unsuitable for travel trailers. He'd discovered some of the outlying train stations had open spots for larger vehicles and with the cameras and bio scanners all over the place, they were extremely secure.

The train dropped him off at the center of a mega structure that served as an office building, shopping mall, and condo complex for several thousand people. Over the past few days, when not in game, or helping the folks at corporate handle the press surrounding Halfworld's main launch, Alan had spent some time making sure he was making the right decision. He'd been wanting to make changes in his life, the travel trailer was a big one, but he was about to make another one.

He glanced at his phone to make sure he was heading the right way. At an average walk, in normal foot traffic, he was only five minutes away. His heart pounded a little faster and he had to keep wiping his hands on his jeans.

Four and a half minutes later, he stepped out of the stream of people moving down the walkway and into the doorway of the shop he was looking for. After the supplies he'd picked up the previous night as he went through Austin, he had everything ready.

There wasn't a door to go through, just an open archway. A short distance from the door a tired-looking middle-aged woman sat behind a counter, staring down like she was looking at either her phone or a tablet.

Alan made it across the clean tile floor before she looked up, probably due to the soft chime that had sounded when he entered the shop.

"Hi, can I help you?" She put down her phone and looked up at him. Dark circles hung under her eyes, and her graying hair was trying to escape the bun she'd put it in.

"Yes, I'm here about this dog." Alan swiped the screen on his phone, sliding the map away and displaying the picture of a large mixed-breed red dog.

"Ah." The woman glanced down and tapped something on a tablet next to her phone. "Are you Alan Gosling?"

"Yes." Alan slipped his phone into his jeans pocket and pulled out his wallet and driver's license. He showed the woman his license.

She nodded. "Thank you. We always want to be sure. It looks like you filled everything out online a couple of days ago. All your info checked out. I am sorry about your house. Same storm that orphaned our boy here."

Alan retuned his license to his wallet and slipped it into his pocket. "Thank you. That was one of the reasons I came down here. I heard a lot of pets had been displaced and orphaned."

"That's good of you. Did you lose a pet in the storm?" She tapped on her tablet some more.

"No." Alan shook his head. "But I'd been thinking about getting one for a while and this seems like the perfect time." Having Wolf in Halfworld had started him thinking, and then when he had gotten out and seen firsthand how bad the devastation had been, he knew he had to help. After donating a couple of thousand from his insurance payout from the house to the Red Cross, he heard about the animals needing homes and started researching.

"You're a good man, Mr. Gosling." She gave him a wide, honest smile. "He's on his way up." She got off her stool and headed around the counter. "If you'd come with me, please. We have special rooms for introductions."

Alan followed her to a small room with a short bench and covered in tile. He debated if he should sit on the bench and wait, or just stay standing there.

The door Alan came through closed, then seconds later another one opened and a woman with a reddish puppy that had markings like a German Shepherd on a red leash walked in. The puppy was four months old, at least according to the listing Alan had seen. He was a ball of energy that rushed up to the lady from the reception desk.

The woman bent over and rubbed the pup for a moment, then it bounded over to Alan.

Squatting down to be closer to the dog's level, Alan reached out a hand the way he'd seen in videos to greet a strange canine. The pup sniffed him twice. There was a subtle difference in the way it felt over the way it felt when Wolf did the same thing in Halfworld, even after Wolf's upgrade to AI. The little bit of reality hit Alan hard. He was going to do this.

The pup jumped up and put its paws on Alan's chest before licking his face. The dog had strong, but not unpleasant breath.

"Red, don't do that." The woman with the leash looked like she was about to put a slight pressure on him.

Alan shook his head. "No. It's okay." He rubbed the pup. "Red huh?"

The pup's tail was going so fast it was nearly swinging around with each whip. His coat was rough and uneven, some of it felt brittle.

"The house he was found near had burned," said the woman with the leash. "The vets had him for nearly six weeks before we got him. He's growing fast and that's helping his coat come back in."

"Yeah." Alan had read that on the puppy's page. His paws had also been burned fairly badly, but had healed to the point that everyone deemed him ready for adoption. "You've been through a rough spot the past couple of months haven't you? I understand."

The puppy sat back on its haunches and tilted its head like it was understanding every word Alan said. He liked the idea the dog was smart. He figured it would be easier to get along with a smart dog IRL than a crazy little fluff ball.

Alan smiled and the puppy launched itself at him again. The motion jerked its leash out of the woman's hand and he nearly knocked Alan over backwards. With a laugh, Alan stood and held the pup in his arms while the armful proceeded to give him a good tongue bath.

"Yeah, I'll take him." Alan knew he would be smart to look at other dogs, but he was determined to get one of the orphaned dogs who had survived the tornado, like he had. There was something special about the big ball of energy in his arms. They would work together and lead each other into new lives that would be a never-ending adventure.

The front desk lady grinned. "Good. There's just a few more pieces of paperwork we need to finalize, and we can get you out the door." She opened the door and headed back into the reception area.

Following her, Alan kept hold of the puppy, not sure he was ready to put him on the floor. It just felt right holding the happy, licky dog.

27

ALAN GOT off the train and carefully led Red over to a grassy spot a short distance from the stairs that led to and from the station. Although the pup had been curious about everything they did on the ride from the rescue to downtown Dallas, he hadn't shown any fear. He was acting like everything was a grand adventure. Alan guessed for him it was. He looked down the block at the imposing bulk of the Total Immersion Systems building that sought to compete with some of the other buildings in the ever-expanding skyline. In many ways, going to corporate HQ was easier than it would've been going back to the call center he and Mike had worked in for years. Since getting out of the game after dealing with Pyranous, he'd been back to the call center once, long enough to clean out the couple of things he wanted from his desk. Although he still worked for the company, he no longer worked there, and it felt good. As a freelance troubleshooter, he was able to go wherever he wanted to and wasn't tied to a desk. As long as he had his pod and access to a network connection he could work from anywhere he wanted.

When he walked into the building, the lady working late shift on the reception desk frowned toward Red, but only said. "Mr. Gosling, they're up on the twentieth floor."

Already knowing that, Alan smiled and nodded. "Thanks." He headed toward the bank of elevators.

Red whined a bit as they entered the glistening steel box, so Alan squatted down to pet him after he tapped the button for 20. It only took a few seconds for the elevator to get them up there and although the takeoff had been easy enough, Alan had to brace himself as the lift came to a stop. With a final scratch between the dog's ears, Alan straightened and was ready to walk out as the door opened.

The party was already in full swing. It was a bit more festive than he'd expected, and there were a lot more people there.

Mike and Lisa came over as he stepped out of the elevator. He shook his head. "You went out and got a puppy. Are you trying to make your real world more game-like?"

Lisa punched him in the arm. "Mike, be nice. He's a cute puppy." She knelt down to pet him and Red bounded over to her. He started licking her face as she glanced up at Alan. "What's his name?"

"At the shelter they were calling him Red. I haven't decided if that's going to stick or not. Give me a couple of days with him and we'll see." He looked past them at all the people there, most of whom he didn't know. "I thought this was going to be our party getting together IRL" He'd met a few of them over the past couple of months, but he been looking forward to getting to know everyone a bit more.

"Blame Rick," Mike said as Lisa stood and Red whined at her feet for more attention. "I think he let it slip to some of the developers that we were doing this. Turns out they all wanted to meet the First Responders too, and then some of them let it slip to the bigwigs and this turned into the official launch party for Halfworld's public release."

Definitely not the party Alan had been expecting. "Why didn't Greensleeves tell me that earlier?" If he had known, he might've put off getting Red for a day so as to not overwhelm the pup.

"Rick probably threatened him if he did." Lisa leaned over and gave Red another round of pets. "They know you'd probably not show up if you'd known."

Alan nodded as David and Rick came over. "Yeah, big parties aren't really my thing."

"And so we kept things quiet." David walked up and pulled Alan into a bear hug. After meeting David a couple of weeks earlier when he'd been driving around the country for a bit of change of scenery, Alan understood where the toon name Bigdaddybear came from. Alan wasn't a small man by anyone's estimate, but David had a good six inches on him, or more, standing over six and a half feet tall, with broad shoulders and a thick, well-trimmed beard. Alan had no doubt that he was rather intimidating in his role as HR head for the Atlanta office. Unlike some of the rest of the guild, he'd opted to keep his regular job when the company was offering them all new jobs as in-game troubleshooters.

"You did a good job at that." Alan said as David put him down, and Rick gave him his own similar warm welcome. At least Rick wasn't as tall as David was and couldn't pick Alan off the ground.

"We're just glad you made it." Rick squatted down and gave Red a quick pet. "So you went ahead and did it." He glanced over at David. "You owe me twenty."

Alan cocked an eyebrow. "What, you two were betting on when I would get a dog?" He wasn't surprised by this, but he didn't realize the couple betted against each other on things.

David pulled out his phone, tapped something on its screen, then laid it against the phone that Rick held out. "Yeah," David said. "I figured it would take you at least six months to break down and get one, and Rick figured it would be less than three. Rick's always better at reading people than I am."

A large African-American woman in a flowing yellow dress laughed as she walked up to them. "And David's in HR." She shook her head. "It's a good thing you play the game so well."

"Shelia, you know how these things go," David said.

"I do." Shelia grinned at them both. "Well, Alan, about time you showed up. I think the big wigs are getting impatient to get the official launch ceremony going."

Alan frowned. "Official ceremony? I thought the official launch took place this morning."

"IRL only," said a tall muscular woman with short brilliant red hair. "They wanna make a big deal in game."

"Mariann?" Alan asked, but he couldn't think of anyone else it could be with the thick Irish accent. She was one of the few First Responder members he hadn't met in real life.

The redhead smiled at him. "An' who else could ah be? Since everybody else has had the decency to introduce themselves, you must be Alan."

"I am." Alan nodded, then offered her his hand.

She shook her head. "Nay, ye're gett'en a hug." She latched on to Alan, and for a moment, he was wondering if she was going to break a rib.

"We're ready," announced a tall slender suit Alan didn't recognize.

"Just in time, Alan," David said. "They're set up and ready for us."

Alan frowned and followed the others to the far side of the room where a bunch of VR goggles and gloves were set up waiting for occupants. At his side Red tucked in tight, like all the people in the room were making him nervous, an emotion Alan completely understood.

On a shimmering disk in the center of the room stood a tall man who looked like he spent more time on a surfboard and beach than he did in a boardroom with his sun-bleached blond hair. His suit looked impeccable and didn't look anything like he did in game.

Alan paused and stared as the man shimmered and flickered. One of the other suits walked up and put his hand through the image.

Slasher frowned. "You know, that'll probably be considered rude at some point in the near future."

"Get used to it. You're top-of-the-line tech at the moment," the other suit replied.

"I guess I am." Slasher frowned. "I only exist as part of programs now." He paused and grinned. "Ah, Alan, you finally made it."

"Sorry, nobody warned me about the big party." Alan looked down at the holographic projector as Red sniffed it. "So this is how they're bringing you out of the game for this." He glanced back at David. "I thought there had been some hints about that."

"Yeah, we were keeping it a surprise. My wife is having the projectors installed all over the house so I can continue to interact with her and the kids." Slasher frowned. "The only problem is they take a ton of power and even with the company paying for them, they can only run so long before they drain the solar and wind batteries. We're talking about getting back on the grid."

A short wispy woman in an expensive suit with her black hair up in a no-nonsense bob walked up. "Mr. Gosling, we've been waiting for you. I don't believe we've ever met. I'm Kim Pin, the new CEO of TES."

Alan gave her a short bow. "It's a pleasure to meet you, Ms. Pin." He'd heard about some changes at the top of the corporate pole in the wake of their adventures, but hadn't bothered to find out all the details.

"You've helped us really understand what our technology can offer our users." Ms. Pin smiled. "There are things you and I should discuss in the coming days." She rubbed Red's head without bending over. "You can even bring this precious puppy if you like. But now, it's time for us to make our entrance."

While they'd been talking, a quiet hush had fallen over the room.

Alan glanced around and most of the people there had gotten VR gear on, only his party was standing there quietly as if waiting for something to happen.

One of the waiters who'd been making sure people had champagne walked up to Alan. "Mr. Gosling, if you'd like, I can walk your dog while you do your duty."

With a bit of reluctance, Alan handed over Red's leash, then squatted down to scratch Red's ears. "You be a good puppy, I'll be back as fast as I can." He hoped he wasn't going to have to spend long in Halfworld. At least they were all using VR goggles and gloves and not pods. There wasn't a chance of him getting stuck in the game again.

"I'll take good care of him," the waiter said as he started leading Red away.

Red glanced from the waiter to Alan and whined softly.

Alan wanted to do whatever the bigwigs wanted to do and get back to the real world and his puppy.

"Here." Mike handed him a set of gear. "Let's do this."

"Yeah." Alan slipped the gloves on, then pulled the goggles over his head.

His launch screen appeared almost instantly. He selected Horc, still his only toon in the game since he'd deleted Horc007, but Rick had made it possible for him to keep the level he'd gotten with 007. He knew Mike and some of the others had rolled up new toons to play when the First Responders didn't have need of them. When he entered the game he wasn't standing outside the guild house in Pyranoville where he'd been earlier when he logged out. He was in the center of Red Wind Terrace.

There was a huge number of toons around him and the others where they stood on a huge wooden platform.

Then Pyranous appeared behind them. The Dragon reared back on his haunches and roared before sending a jet of flame into the air.

People screamed, then clapped as the flames died out harmlessly.

Ms. Pin, in game as a Gnome Mage, waved her hands around, creating a huge fireworks display around them before her voice boomed out. "Welcome to Halfworld, everyone!"

There was more applause and Pyranous sent another flaming display into the twilight sky.

Horc had to admit that if he was going to go to a big game release party, he liked the idea of it being in-game better than IRL any day. Somewhere nearby, a band started up and people started dancing. It was a far cry from the way things could've been. There was still a lot of the game Horc had to explore, but he had all the time in the world to do that. The fantasy world was much more than he ever expected it to be, and if what he'd been told by Rick, the designers were working on being able to get new content out as fast as possible. There would always be something new and interesting to explore. That made Horc feel good about the future.

Titanya and Greensleeves each grabbed one of his arms.

"Come on, you're going to dance and enjoy this before the next emergency comes up," Greensleeves said.

"Exactly." Titanya patted him on the arm. "We're the First Responders. We party hard, and we save the world."

Horc hoped the world would go for a while without needing saving, but when it did again, he and his guild would be there, ready to give it their all.

The End…for now
Be sure to look for "The Return of Horc" in 2019

If you'd like to stay on top of new releases and upcoming
work by Drew Seren, please join our mailing list. Sign up
at www.drewseren.com
And if you enjoyed Horc's third adventure, please leave a
review. It's easy and won't take you very long.

DREW SEREN
Drew Seren Bio

Drew Seren was raised on a diet of science fiction, both in print and on the screen. He spent many nights watching Star Trek and Space 1999 with his father. Comic books were a main staple of his reading, and then when he was in high school he started reading *Dragon Riders of Pern* and quickly began devouring any science fiction he could, luckily his father had an extensive library at the time. He started writing soon after that, letting writing help him make it through class. During college and his corporate life, Drew spent a lot of time writing to help him endure the mundane things that gnawed at him. Through his twenties and thirties, comic books and science fiction helped him survive. To this day, he's still reading as much or more than he's writing. He's also an avid gamer, playing first *Dungeons and Dragons*, and currently lots of *World of Warcraft*. He's recently turned his attention to writing full time and exploring the vast galaxy through new and interesting eyes.

Stay in touch with Drew through his website
www.drewseren.com

and Facebook pages
fb.me/drewseren

Feel free to drop me an email
drew@drewseren.com

www.ingramcontent.com/pod-product-compliance
Lightning Source LLC
Chambersburg PA
CBHW071155180726
48291CB00007B/2468

With This Wish

Trent Sinclair knows love and loss. He holds both close to his heart and private. But when he meets Lilly McCall, the sister of his brother-in-law, suddenly his life is turned upside down.

Lilly McCall has been running from her past as long as she can remember. She keeps busy helping out at one national park after the other...but now her past is catching up to her and she's come to Windswept Bay looking for answers. She isn't counting on the handsome, quiet Trent Sinclair turning her world upside down and putting her wounded heart on the line.

Don't miss this next heartwarming, touching story in the Windswept Bay Series~the sisters have had their love stories now its time for the brothers to get swept away by love.